First Mercy
Then Grace

*Care for the children
they are Gods gift.*

First Mercy Then Grace

VIRGINIA J. FLO

CROSSBOOKS
PUBLISHING

CrossBooks™
A Division of LifeWay
1663 Liberty Drive
Bloomington, IN 47403
www.crossbooks.com
Phone: 1-866-879-0502

First published by CrossBooks 6/24/2011

ISBN: 978-1-6150-7890-5 (sc)
ISBN: 978-1-6150-7891-2 (hc)

Library of Congress Control Number: 2011929553

Printed in the United States of America

This book is printed on acid-free paper.

*To my parents, who opened their home
to many foster children, showing by example
their faith and family values.*

CHAPTER 1

Samuel was in the field plowing. He wondered what Ruth was doing as he hadn't seen her for hours. He was on the other end of their 80 acres trying to expand what was to be a cornfield. The only way to get ahead was to keep expanding. He just hoped he could handle the additional work involved in adding more fields. He had the land. He just had to make it usable. It was hard work but he was certainly happy to have a tractor and two-bottom plow. Now he could plow two rows at a time. It was much better than the horse and hand plow his father used when he ran his farm. Samuel had opened up an additional five acres last year and it wasn't that hard so this year he was making the attempt to clear ten more.

It was that time of year when he had the planting all done and was waiting for things to start growing. It was a short window of opportunity but he had to try. If he didn't get it accomplished there was always next year, at least that's what he kept telling himself. If he didn't get this new ten acres planted soon it would be too late into the growing season and his plants might not mature before harvest. If that happened his money for the seed would be wasted and they couldn't afford that. All he could do was to try. Ruth was always so encouraging. She made him feel like he could do anything and that's all the encouragement he needed to keep him going. He wondered often why the Lord blessed him with a wife that was so supportive. Why did he wait so long before he decided that marriage was for him?

He thought about Ruth a lot during his daily work. He loved her even though he didn't say it. He hoped she understood and could figure it out by the way he treated her. It just was so hard for him to express his feelings. He did worry about Ruth and how hard she worked. In spite of their meager means and hard work they were blessed with two wonderful daughters, Martha and Rachel. They were the joy of their lives. But, sons were not to be had. He wondered if all of his hard work would mean he'd have a farm without the help of a son to share the satisfaction he felt in owning and working his own farm. Ruth never complained but he knew the hard work had taken its toll as she had three miscarriages during their few years of marriage. They rarely discussed it yet he felt certain the work was the main cause of Ruth's struggles with having children. She, of course, wouldn't hear of it.

He didn't share the belief that you could only pass the farm on to sons. Yet, having only girls made him think about it often. What if their husbands had their own family farm to run and it wasn't close enough to make it practical to combine them. What if their husbands didn't want the farm? After all, Ruth's younger brother didn't want to farm so he left to do something else. Ruth wasn't getting any younger and continuing to put her through the risk of losing babies was not something he wanted to see her endure. It took its toll on him as well, as he loved children and felt such a deep loss when these tragedies happened.

They always hoped things would get easier. That would not prove to be the case. Samuel and Ruth led a simple life, farming. Living off the land was all they knew. A lot of hard work, long hours and perseverance were built into their very being. It was spring of 1952 and they had been married for ten years. All Samuel wanted was a better life than his parents, which was filled with adversities and financial struggles.

Ruth and Samuel had both sacrificed much for their families. They both stayed at home to work their parent's farms, being the last to leave. They found themselves into their thirties before they wed. People might have thought they were leftovers that came together out of convenience but they truly found love in their union.

Samuel's family emigrated from Germany. His parents came over in the late 1890's. They met and married in the United States. Following other family members to Minnesota they came for an opportunity to farm the fertile land they had heard so much about. They were told the land was abundant and ready for the picking. Had that been true Samuel's family would not have struggled as they did to simply make ends meet?

His father didn't own his own farm, rather he rented, and they did all they could to just survive. That is why when Samuel started his own venture, renting with the option to buy, was ideal for his situation. He felt so fortunate to find this farm whose owners, the Wagner brothers, were getting older and wanted to retire from farming. It had been a family farm with the two brothers and their wives working it. Since it was only 80 acres it wasn't big enough to support two families so one of the brothers and his wife had already moved to town and was working at the grain elevator. Neither of these brothers had children to pass the farm to so selling was their best option.

Samuel got to know the Wagner family years ago when he did odd jobs and helped with their harvest. He stayed in touch hoping that someday he might have a chance to purchase their farm. In this area it was rare for farms to come up for sale. As he got to know them he was treated very kindly, almost like a son. So, they certainly were happy he was willing to take on the challenge when they finally decided it was time to move to town.

The town was a small place called Greenville. It had a grocery store called Bartlett's, owned by the Bartlett brothers Ben and Matthew, where Samuel both sold to and purchased groceries. The Bartlett's treated the farmers especially well, as they both needed each other to operate. George Adams, the town's former blacksmith ran the hardware store. Hilda and Gerald Gruber, a nice couple who were especially kind to all of the children in the community, operated the drug store, which also served as a general store. They carried clothing and other household goods that farmers might need in a hurry and couldn't take the time to drive to the big city.

Greenville was located just southwest of St. Paul, the state capital of Minnesota. They were located close enough to the big city that many of the locals had relatives who moved there when they left the farm. West St. Paul, a sprawling suburb, was a haven for retired farmers looking for the conveniences of the city while still keeping as close as possible to the country. Ruth's parents moved to West St. Paul a few years ago, when her father developed a heart condition and had to leave farming. Just last year he passed away from a heart attack and her mother now lives there alone.

Greenville has a railroad track running right through town. The train stops at the grain elevator and transports the grain and corn to St. Paul. There it is either loaded onto a barge heading down the Mississippi River or it continues on to Minneapolis, better known as the "mill" city, where it will be sold to one of the mills for processing. Ruth and Samuel are in the right place and both of them feel all they need is a little hard work, along with the Lord's continued blessings, and things will work out for them.

Their farm came with a big old farmhouse plus a smaller house next door. Samuel's father and mother moved in to the small house, as they could no longer sustain their own livelihood, especially with Samuel leaving. Even if Samuel would have stayed their farm was not producing enough for them to keep up with the rent. Something had to happen and getting this new start was best for all of them. Both of his parents were aging and his mother's health was failing. His father helped the best he could to ease the burden that Samuel and Ruth took on as they started with nothing except a strong desire to succeed. They couldn't afford to hire help so whatever his father could do was appreciated.

There was one thing his father was able to give his son, which was a small herd of milk cows. For this contribution Samuel gave his parents the little house next door that came with the farm. A few more milk cows, some chickens, pigs and beef cattle came with the farm. Samuel and Ruth now had a real dairy farm. They planned to add more as they could afford them. Right now they were thankful for credit, as without it they would be in the same circumstances as Samuel's folks with no cash flow to keep things going. They wouldn't have qualified at the bank but the brothers who sold them the farm were willing to finance it with little down payment. The Wagner brothers had saved for their retirement and the payments Ruth and Samuel made each month were all they needed to be comfortable. They seemed just happy to sell the farm to people who would keep it going in the manner they thought it should run. They were pleased to sell to the Schultz's rather than sell off pieces of the farm to neighboring farmers and lose the essence of what they had worked so hard to build. So, the sale to Samuel and Ruth was a mutual arrangement.

Samuel would watch his father put in a full days work trying to make up for his lack of being able to pass on a working farm to his only son. He worked tirelessly taking on as many duties as Samuel would allow him to do and he could physically handle. Samuel's only sibling was his older sister, Esther, who had years before married Walter, a local farmer. They didn't have children so they were devoted to Martha and Rachel. A birthday or holiday didn't go by without Esther making something special for the girls. She was Rachel's godmother so she might have tended to her just a little bit more but not enough for Martha to realize the difference.

Ruth's parents were second-generation immigrants also coming from Germany, only 20 years earlier than Samuel's parents, when the land was more available. They were able to purchase rather than rent and by all standards, at the time, were considered well to do. She had four siblings, three brothers and a sister. In Ruth's parent's time, it was traditional that the sons would inherit the family farm. The daughters were expected to marry into another family with their own farm. Since Ruth hadn't found a proper suitor until she was 30 she was the last to marry of her siblings. Although she was the second youngest she was the last to leave the farm. Her younger bother was off to do anything but farming as soon as he was of age. Her father had already given her older brothers portions of the family farm when they got married and they ended up with the rest of it after their father retired.

Somehow it didn't seem right. Ruth had worked hard on her father's farm. She plowed the fields, with the use of horses, milked cows, worked the fields during harvest, planted the vegetable garden, fed and tended to all of the animals and whatever else her father asked her to do. Plus she was expected to assist her mother with the housework including cleaning, and cooking, as that was the duty of any daughter with the expectation it would make her a good wife. As a result of all this she certainly knew the meaning of hard work and was willing to work side by side with Samuel in the fields and in the barn while still completing her domestic duties.

On this day Ruth had planned to butcher chickens so they would have food in their freezer for the next few months. Plus they had orders for butchered chickens from their customers on their egg route, which they delivered weekly. That was a big job that would last a good portion of the day. Samuel was thinking that by now, since it was close to noon, she would have gotten the water boiling after cleaning up from breakfast and probably had gathered all of the chickens to be butchered into a separate pen. Ruth was efficient at doing this task, as she had done it many times before. Living on the farm required such duties and they were just something you did when living off the land.

Samuel was anxious to go home for lunch to see how Ruth was doing. He knew she probably had also taken a break from her endeavor to make lunch so when he got there it would be ready to eat. He couldn't afford to take too much time for lunch, as he needed to get back into the field and go as far as he could as long as there was daylight. He looked at his pocket watch and it was about eleven fifteen. He thought he would work until eleven thirty and then start home. When he got home he would fill the tractor with gasoline and also fill the spare cans with gas to take with him to the field so he didn't have to make a trip home just to refuel. By then it would be noon and he knew Ruth would be expecting him at the table.

He loved his wife and his two young daughters so much. He was proud of his family and wanted to be the best husband and father he could be. He loved what he was doing as he felt a certain excitement in being able to provide for his young family as well as helping his parents, who now also depended on the farm.

Even with all of their excitement in being able to start their own farm, Samuel felt guilty every time Ruth would join him in the farm work. Yet, he knew he had to accept it because he could not afford to hire help. It required Ruth's assistance in order to grow their herd and maximize their harvests. They both wanted to make it past the first few years of renting and exercise their option to buy the farm. This common goal kept them focused and willing to make sacrifices to make it come to fruition.

Samuel felt a strong devotion to his faithful and loving wife. He knew she felt the same way as she demonstrated each and every day of their lives. Their struggles for survival grew their love for each other. They both had a strong Christian faith that continued to grow as they both relied on the Lord to provide for them. They were extremely thankful for what they considered many blessings in their lives. Love for each other and faith in the Lord was their mainstay.

CHAPTER 2

Ruth's morning had been very busy. After breakfast was done and she said good-bye to Samuel the children woke up. They were ready to take on the world with their excitement about what they might do and how much fun they would have that day. She served them breakfast and took a few minutes for a second cup of coffee to listen to their chatter. After all, when you are three and six you have a lot to say and things that must be told. She smiled as she listened. They knew what Ruth was going to be doing. They had seen this event enough that they were certain they could help.

Ruth listened intently to their request to help but knew this would be no work for two very young children. Perhaps they could pluck a few feathers to appease their curiosity but at best that would be the extent of it. Never could they catch these feathered creatures nor could they end their lives. Perhaps that would even be difficult for them to watch, even though this was a routine part of farm life. Yes, Ruth thought, perhaps she would let them share in plucking duties after she dipped them in hot water to loosen the feathers. She just needed to be careful that she kept the down feathers. She was saving them so someday, when she had enough, she would make down pillows for her two daughter's hope chests.

The whole process of butchering chickens was tedious and time consuming. She thought it was a good thing she had her mother-in-law there to watch the children so she could concentrate on the task and not have to worry about what the girls were doing. Ruth was especially protective of her two girls as when they were born she was so incredibly grateful to have carried them to full term. She lost a baby before and after Martha and one more after Rachel's birth. Ever since, she asks for the Lord's help, to keep both of them safe forever. She would never forget what a blessing they were to Samuel and her.

After feeding the children and getting them busy playing with their dolls in the living room, she ran next door to ask her mother-in-law to come over and sit with the girls while they played. It didn't take long, as her mother-in-law was up early waiting for Ruth's call. She was prepared for her predetermined day's assignment. Watching the girls was something she did almost every day and so looked forward to it, as she loved her two young granddaughters with all her heart. Being frail, with a heart condition, she had to take it easy and although keeping up with two young children could be challenging she never lost interest in doing it. Since Samuel's parents small home was right next door to the main farmhouse it took less than five minutes for his mother to respond to Ruth's request.

Ruth then went out to the chicken coop and gathered up about ten chickens she had intended to butcher and put them in a smaller fenced area. There they would be easily accessible to her when she was ready to begin the job. No point in these ten filling up their gizzards with chicken feed that would later go to waste. She knew she wouldn't be able to get to the butchering process until after lunch, as her daily duties needed to be done first. She also wanted to make lunch so it would be ready promptly when Samuel arrived home.

As she did her work that morning, which included gathering the eggs, feeding the chickens, geese and pigs she thought about when she and Samuel would begin the process of purchasing the farm, which was quickly approaching. She could only focus on how far they had come from their meager beginnings. They basically had started with the small head of cattle from her father-in-law, some used machinery in need of repair and a few things her brother had given them as outdated equipment he no longer used. And, here they were ready to take the next step by actually purchasing the land and buildings. Without the Lord blessing their dedication and hard work, this would not have been possible. The Lord must have granted them success because they certainly had nothing to start with and they both knew they weren't worthy. It had to have been a heavenly gift.

Her chores were done and now she was making lunch. It was important on the farm that the noon meal was sufficient to carry farmers through the rest of the day so it was always one of substance. She often included her in-laws in the noon meal as they were generally with them helping with the chores. Today her father-in-law was cleaning the barn and starting the process of whitewashing the walls, something they had to do to keep the areas where they milked clean and sanitary. Not an easy job but one that her father-in-law was willing to do. So, everyone had his or her task in this routine day on the farm.

Today she was making a special treat for everyone. Their family loved to go to one of several local lakes and fish. They did just that a few days earlier and she was now frying up some of the fish they caught. She made a combination of sunfish and bullheads. Both very different but much enjoyed by all. She already boiled the potatoes, made some cabbage slaw and cooked some corn as their vegetable. Yesterday she baked fresh bread and also made coffee cake, which they would have for dessert.

While she fried the fish she looked out the window and saw Samuel coming across the field driving his old Case tractor pulling the plow behind. She figured she had about twenty minutes by the time he got to the shed, filled the tractor with gasoline, got to the house and cleaned up. By then she would have the meal on the table, with the children seated with their grandparents ready to say grace. She smiled as she saw Samuel. She loved seeing him. He had a great big smile that he used as he entered the house and greeted his family. It brought such joy to her heart, as she knew that for all of those years when she waited for the right person that she did indeed find him.

Everyone was gathered in the kitchen. It was the largest room in the house. It had a large counter with a sink, a stove and refrigerator and a huge table with 6 big chairs around it. Even Rachel sat in a big chair, as she wanted no part of her high chair when she turned three. A few Sears catalogs under her and she could reach the table, like everyone else.

Samuel came in from outside and stopped to remove his shoes, gloves and jacket on the porch right off the kitchen. In he came and everyone perked up. And there was that huge smile which went from ear to ear, no holding back. The girls couldn't contain themselves as they raced across the room yelling "Daddy, Daddy" each grabbing a leg as they reached him. He patted them on their backs and heads and told them to take their seats, as he would be right back. He then walked into the bathroom, right off the kitchen, bringing them along for a step or two until they finally released him.

It didn't take him long and he was back in the kitchen ready to eat. Everyone was now seated, except Ruth. She always waited to see if Samuel needed anything else before she sat down. Neither of them showed a lot of outward affection except the smiles and glimmer in their eyes as they exchanged loving glance before sitting down. Showing affection openly just wasn't their style. They certainly were affectionate to their children they just didn't do it to each other, at least in the presence of others. But, one could see they were very content with each other and always happy to see one another. If they were trying to hide their joy in being together they weren't doing a very good job of it.

Saying grace was a family affair and it consisted of the common table prayer. And now they said it together led by Samuel.

"Come Lord Jesus, be our guest. And, let these gifts to us be blessed".

Even the children joined in, as no meal would begin without saying grace. This was much more than tradition; it was a way of life. Never did Samuel and Ruth lose sight of the blessings they had received and always expressed their gratitude to God.

The meal would start with the men telling about their morning. That is, of course, if they could get ahead of the children. The girls had, however, learned at an early age to be respectful of their elders. So, if one of the adults was speaking they did try and hold back their stories, even though they couldn't always help themselves due to their excitement. Living on the farm gave them a great deal to talk about. There was never a moment when some adventure took place where they weren't using their imagination in telling the story. This day they had played with their dolls most of the morning so, they seemed content to let the adults speak.

Samuel's father spoke first with a bit of German mixed in, "Ya, I got half done in the barn dis morning. Da cats might have gotten white wash on dem, as day just wouldn't stay away. Serves dem right, we just got too many of dem critters."

He didn't have a lot of patience for any animals that didn't provide milk or food. Yet, he did appreciate the cats keeping the mice population down and away from the cattle's food.

Samuel went next saying "I think I'll be able to finish plowing the north field today if I stay with it. Not as many rocks to pick, as I was worried about and it's going much faster than I thought. That way, in the next few days I can disc it and we might just have the making of another ten acres to plant this year."

Ruth looked on with much pride in her husband as he spoke. She was always so proud of him.

Samuel then added "I'm think it was the right thing to do in also planting more vegetables this year. I can take more to market when they are ripe. It seems to be a popular thing these days for the city folk to purchase those fresh vegetables. They want the fresh grown stuff rather than that trucked in stuff they get at the grocery store. I'm going to talk to Bob at Bartlett's to see if he might buy some of our vegetables. I know he already purchases from some other farmers but why not us? It might be a long shot but I'm going to try. Maybe it will bring a better price than the corn and oats we plant every year. I was hoping that if I can get the added ten acres of corn planted it would give us a little extra cash to use over the winter. I'm just not sure I'll get it planted in time to be able to harvest it. If I can't get the field ready in a couple of weeks, which will already be June, I'm not spending money on seed as I don't want to take the risk."

Samuel's father added, "Dat would be a good idea not to vaste da seed. You can alvays plant dat ten acres next year."

Samuel's mother rarely joined in these table conversations and just nodded her approval from time to time as others spoke. Samuel then asked Ruth what she did this morning. She told of getting the chickens ready and how she had successfully fed all of the animals. Ruth wasn't one for going on about things so she stopped abruptly and went back to eating.

Samuel then changed the subject, "these fish are great. I'm so happy we took a half-day this week and went fishing. I know it took away from our fieldwork but now we have fresh fish and food in the freezer for more meals."

That comment opened the door for the girls to rethink their day at the lake. They both had different stories that were being told at the same time until Ruth asked them to stop talking and eat their food. Everyone loved the fish. The girls usually got the bullheads as they had much larger bones and made it easier for them to eat. Ruth would also remove the bones from a small sunfish so they could have a taste. Everyone now settled in and finished their meal. At the end of the meal they always gave thanks again for the food.

Together they said, "Oh give thanks unto the Lord for He is good and His mercy endures forever, Amen".

Everyone quietly got up from the table and went their own way to begin the afternoon tasks. Ruth then cleared the table, along with the help of her mother-in-law. They washed and wiped the dishes leaving no dirty dish around for the next meal. Leftovers were rare, as the two men would usually clean up anything left. On this day she did have some cooked corn left, which she refrigerated and would use again at another meal. She was thinking, as she put it in the refrigerator, maybe it was time to make some chicken soup. She still had a lot of vegetables in cold storage in the basement and they should be used up before the next harvest. Yes, she would make chicken soup using the left over corn once her chickens were butchered.

CHAPTER 3

*I*t was now evening and all of the afternoon chores were done. Samuel did complete his work in tilling the new ten acres that hadn't been tilled for sometime. Ruth cleaned her ten chickens and they were now safely in the refrigerator. With the exception of one she kept for tomorrow's chicken soup they were all wrapped carefully ready to deliver to customers on their next egg route.

Supper was over, the table was cleared and Ruth removed the tablecloth so Samuel could do his bookwork. This was a ritual that took place once a week. It was important to stay on top of their finances. Money was tight and making certain their cash flow was staying in the black was very important.

As Samuel worked his way through the bills and looked at his milk check and the money from their egg route, he said to Ruth, "All we need is just a little more each month and we could make it without such a struggle."

At that comment Ruth perked up and came over to the table and sat down next to Samuel. She began to talk getting more excited as she went.

"I have been talking with some of the ladies at church, Samuel. They said that there are people from farms in our area that are taking in foster children from St. Paul. There seems to be a feeling that getting some of these children from troubled homes into the country could help them. They need to get away from the big city to a more simple life, which is what we have. Samuel, if we were to take a child or two we would get paid for it, which could help us financially. We have such a large house with so many bedrooms that remain empty most of the time."

"Wait, wait a minute Ruth", Samuel replied, "We haven't spoken of this before, when did you hear this? Who is telling you this?"

"I was speaking to Pastor Hadley and his wife. They thought it might be good for us to have another child in our house. Maybe it could even be a boy. What if it was an older boy? He could even work with you on the farm. I'm not talking about getting a foster child so they could work the farm. I thought they might get enjoyment out of being on the farm and doing the things that we get such joy in doing."

She was starting to talk faster trying to get every word in before she knew she could get cut off. Samuel wasn't saying no so she was encouraged. She was trying to give him some selling points that might interest him.

Samuel sat in his chair for a while speechless. Where was this coming from, he thought? Was this Ruth's way of dealing with losing the children she did? Perhaps it was. He also felt a loss and emptiness in not having all the children they wanted. Would this work for them? Not the money, but filling their void. Maybe it could.

Finally, he spoke, "Is this what you would like to do? What do we have to do to get started?"

Before he had a chance to say another word Ruth spoke up saying, "We need to call the welfare department in Ramsey County since that county is the one with the greatest need. They will send someone out to sign us up and check us out. Pastor Hadley said he could help and would recommend us. Apparently there is quite a shortage. It is really sad to hear there are so many children in need of foster homes. My heart goes out to them. Samuel, I've been thinking about this for sometime and I really would like us to look into doing this."

"Okay", he said, "Let's see what needs to be done. It doesn't hurt to talk with them. If we can offer something to help a young child that would certainly be a good thing. Do you know who to call?"

"Yes" she said, "I got the number from someone in town who already does this. I hope that was okay, Samuel. I didn't want to do something behind your back but I needed to know more about this before I decided I'd like to do it and tell you about it. After talking with that lady I know now we have what it takes to be a good foster family. And, Samuel, I think this is the Lord's Will. We lost our precious babies and this might just be a way the Lord has in mind to give us something in return."

"Now Ruth, you know that foster children would be here on a temporary basis and you can't get attached to them as they won't be our own. From what I have heard this isn't just about children who have lost both parents. Sometimes children are taken away from their parents and when their parents get their lives back in order the children go back."

Samuel was starting to get concern about her words and didn't want her to get hurt all over again with losing a child.

"I know" Ruth responded. "This is about helping children. If it also can help us, what harm can that do? Maybe it will be hard but I'm willing to give it a try. Does this mean you agree to give it a try as well?"

"Okay, I said, let's check it out", Samuel responded, "You give the person a call and set up a meeting, let's see what this is all about."

It was amazing that the two of them had this much time to talk without their girls stopping by to get their attention. They were coloring on the dining room table and that was keeping them occupied for the moment. Now the moment was up and Martha appeared in the dining room doorway.

"Mommy", she said, can we have a glass of milk?"

"Of course you can", Ruth said as she got right up and walked to the refrigerator. As she got up she glanced back and made eye contact with Samuel as to say *'thank you for supporting me in this'*.

All Ruth could think about all evening was how it would be to have more children in their house. As she put the girls to bed the same thoughts were still in her mind as she had so much love to give these children she couldn't even explain it.

As she tucked them in Martha said, "Mommy, why are you so quiet? Are you sick?"

"Oh no", Ruth answered back, "I am not sick. I am just thinking about how wonderful you both are and how great it would be to have more children in this big house."

Now Martha too was quiet pondering all that she just heard. Most of this was way too complicated for Rachel who was just waiting to say her bedtime prayer.

"Let's say our prayers now, okay?" Ruth suggested.

And, so the two girls began to pray, "Now I lay me down to sleep, I pray the Lord my soul to keep. If I should die before I wake, I pray the Lord my soul to take. And this I ask for Jesus sake."

Each and every time Ruth heard these two little ones pray that prayer, she felt the comfort in knowing that the Lord had taken care of her little ones who didn't make it into this world. What a fitting reminder to have this special prayer recited each and every evening by her two young daughters.

When Ruth lost her first baby the Lord was merciful and helped her deal with the loss by bringing her comfort and peace in the knowledge that He is a merciful God. She felt certain her baby was with the Lord. He then showed his powerful grace by giving her Martha, whose birth gave her great joy. God was again merciful when she lost her second baby and again through prayer she was able to cope. Without God's never-ending mercy, she didn't know how she would have been able to endure a second loss.

When Rachel arrived the grace of God showed vividly in her life once more. After Rachel was born they were uncertain about becoming pregnant again but they so wanted a son to compliment their family. After much prayer they decided to try one more time with the hope that the Lord would bless them with a son. When they experienced their third loss both Ruth and Samuel knew they dared not try another time.

They had no desire to see another life ended and the risk was too high. How would God show his grace, after that final loss when perhaps they shouldn't have tried again? That was their ongoing question and only through God's mercy were they able to accept their fate.

As Ruth watched her two daughters fall asleep, she wondered if the gift of having foster children was God's new act of grace. Her faith was strong and both she and Samuel were willing to take in these unknown children. She was certain they were in need of the love and kindness both she and Samuel were capable of giving. Although their lives together were full of struggles, she knew when they put their lives into God's hands the outcome was first mercy then grace.

She finished tucking the girls in and now went to her own bedroom, where Samuel was already getting ready for bed. Farmers went to bed early, as they also got up early to do their milking chores. As the sun came up and sometimes even before, so did they.

Samuel and Ruth were very quiet, as they got ready for bed. Samuel cradled Ruth in his arm as they both laid down, neither of them saying a word. It took a while for both of them to fall asleep as they had much to think about. Tomorrow would be a new day that would change their lives forever. Sleep did come and they both slept amazingly sound. The Lord blest that night with calm and that was the best blessing he could have given them.

CHAPTER 4

*T*he next day came quickly. Quiet still permeated throughout the house as Ruth and Samuel were starting their duties for this new day. It was a glorious spring morning. The sun was starting to come up and there was a small breeze coming from the southwest. There was just a little chill in the air but with the warm breeze it was destine to warm up soon.

Ruth quickly fried up a few eggs with a slice of ham for Samuel before he went to the barn for milking. Sometimes he would wait until after milking to have his breakfast but this morning Ruth made certain he was fed before he started his busy day. He sat down while Ruth grabbed the toast and coffee pot to complete the meal.

As she sat down putting the coffee pot on the table Samuel said, "I'll say grace this morning."

Expecting him to say the common prayer Ruth folded her hands, bowed her head and waited for the familiar words.

Samuel started with a little hesitation and then just kept moving forward. "Dear Lord, we..ah..ah..thank you for this food..ah..that you have provided for us."

Ruth was surprised, as he never deviated from the common table prayer.

Yet he continued, "Lord, we have been blessed with many things and for that we are thankful. We just want to ask you to continue to be with us and guide us in this new thing we are about to do. Help us to do the right thing. And, if you want us to help children in need then so be it. We will take your lead in this. Please show us the way. In Jesus name we pray. Amen."

Ruth added another "Amen" and the prayer was over.

Without saying a word, they both picked up a knife to butter their toast that Ruth had put in front of them when she sat down. Ruth couldn't help but glance up at him still wondering about his prayer. Samuel had such a difficult time saying how he felt but, what a wonderful prayer that expressed such feeling. He was hard to understand but it was great to have him as her husband.

They finished eating and together they closed with "Oh give thanks unto to the Lord for He is good, and His mercy endures forever. Amen".

It seemed to have a little more meaning this time. With a smile on both of their faces they now went their separate ways, Samuel to the barn and Ruth to the sink to do the breakfast dishes. Each one filled with a wonderful spirit of joy that just couldn't be explained. They were seriously planning on having more children in their home. They certainly both had room in their hearts and lots of love to share. Had their dreams of more children finally come true even though the gifts would be with them only temporarily? It would have to be enough for now.

It would be a while until the girls woke. Ruth enjoyed this time of day when she had a few moments alone in complete silence. It was her time to do whatever she wanted to do for herself. She thought it was ironic because even though she could now do something for herself she often used this time to do things for others. Maybe she would be darning socks or making new clothes for the girls. This morning was a little different. She sat down and jotted down a few notes about what she would say when she called the welfare department. She tried to anticipate what they might ask. She wanted to be ready for anything. After she had a list of about a dozen possible things to say she ran out of time. She could hear the shuffle of little feet in the upstairs hallway headed for the stairs.

The girls got up with lots of energy, had their breakfast and were soon outside using their imagination to find ways to play in ways that entertained their inquisitive minds. Ruth was busy by now feeding the animals, and trying to hold back her excitement. This was the day she could finally call the social worker at the welfare department about being a foster mother. She had finally gotten the courage to ask Samuel and he agreed. She just was so excited she could hardly focus on her chores.

It was mid morning and she could now make that infamous call. She headed toward the house. Making the call was not at all as she had expected. She was put through to a Mrs. Adams right away. As soon as she said she lived in the country on a farm Mrs. Adams asked when she could come and visit. They set up a time for the next day and the call was over. It went so quickly she actually felt a little let down when she hung up. After she thought about it, she realized that there was a little excitement in Mrs. Adams voice and she was very quick to ask for an appointment. Ruth thought that was a good thing and hoped it was.

The next day they were all sitting on pins and needles waiting for Mrs. Adams to arrive. They had told Anna and Gerhardt, Samuel's parents, the whole story the night before. Although they were happy for Samuel and Ruth, both were concerned that they would be terribly disappointed when these children would leave their care and go back home, as many of them did. They knew how hurt Samuel and Ruth had been when they lost their babies and certainly didn't want to see them endure that again. But, they would be supportive and also be there for them, if they were needed.

Ruth was also able to reach her mother by phone and share the news. She was, of course, also happy for them but shared the same concerns as Anna and Gerhardt. By phone it was a little more difficult to have a good conversation. Ruth said she would let her know once they were told they qualified. She missed having her mother close by. She would have loved to sit down and talk with her about many things. After all, she spent so much of her life doing just that and she missed it.

After gathering the girls to share the news, Ruth was first to begin talking; "We have been told that there are some children who may not have parents to take care of them, like you do. They need to find a place to stay until new parents are found to care for them. We have offered to let them stay with us until they find their new home."

Samuel added quickly, before the children could speak, "We know that Jesus would want us to help others because we have a home and a family and in sharing this with other children we would be doing a good thing."

The children were a little confused, being as young as they were, but accepted the prospect of having more children with which to play.

Martha asked, "Who are these children? Where are they coming from? Why don't they have a home of their own?"

Rachel was too young to understand although she did sit quietly and listen as they were being told.

Ruth responded, "Sometimes parent die or are sick or having difficult times before their children are old enough to care for themselves."

Martha interrupted, "Are you going to die?"

"No, no", Samuel chimed in. "But, there are times when families have to go through some bad things. Yet, you know that Jesus is always there to help them. Having them come and live with us for a while is one of the ways Jesus is helping."

Ruth added, "Remember that picture of Jesus holding those children that you like so well from Sunday School?"

Martha nodded her head in agreement. Rachel also nodded.

"Well, that picture of Jesus represents how we are supposed to be. He said we are to welcome little children because when we do it's like welcoming him. He expects us to hold the children who need holding for him and he watches over us when we do it."

By this time both Martha and Rachel were moving closer to Samuel and Ruth who both put their arms around them and did indeed hold them close.

"We may become foster parents", Ruth continued, "It will be our job to foster or take care of children for a time, until they are ready to go on to another family or go back to their own family. You will be foster sisters to these children and we will treat them as if they are part of our family."

Samuel asked, "Do you think you can do that?"

Both girls were pondering all of this with a questioning look. Ruth and Samuel were hoping they had heard what they had said and would understand.

Martha then said one more thing that brought a tear to the eyes of Ruth and Samuel, "Does this mean we can have a brother?"

Ruth and Samuel were overwhelmed. Was she aware of their emotional roller coaster or was she simply asking for herself? Either way, it was certainly profound.

"Maybe", Samuel said, "Maybe we will. We also might just get another girl who is just as cute as both of you."

He then tickled them and they both giggled as they went back to their dollhouse, where they had been playing. All Ruth and Samuel could do was to look at each, as there weren't words to explain how they felt. Raising children was indeed a joy, this little conversation proved it.

Mrs. Adams did come out and interview their family. She even talked with Samuel's parents. They completed all of the appropriate paperwork and now they were waiting for everything to be processed. The same questions kept running through their minds. Would they be approved? If they were, what child would they be given? Would they be good foster parents? It was difficult for them to keep their routine. Things went from running in high gear to going in slow motion. They were simply in a waiting pattern as it was now totally out of their control. They needed to find some sense of normality so they could continue.

Fortunately, it had now advanced to Sunday. It was a great way to bring some peace back into their lives. Going to church and Sunday School was a wonderful way to refresh their spirits and stay close to the Lord. It helped to get things back into perspective. Raising their voices to praise the Lord in song, hearing a sermon that happened to be about the blessings of family and listening to the Word being spoken was just what they needed. They could now go on whether or not the foster parent opportunity was given to them. Heading back home, they were at peace and realized that Samuel's prayer earlier in the week, where he asked the Lord to guide them, was now actually happening. Knowing that the Lord was doing the leading was the assurance they needed in knowing what they were about to do was the right thing for them. Is this what the Lord had in mind for them all along through their struggles in having children? Were they supposed to be foster parents to lots of children rather than just their own? Having Martha and Rachel gave them a good start and now they were ready to take their lives to the next level.

CHAPTER 5

It was now Monday morning around nine o'clock. Ruth was gathering all of the laundry for her Monday washing and the phone rang. She had to catch her breath before she picked up the phone. The anticipation might now be over and she was a little frightened at the prospect of being turned down.

The phone kept ringing and she knew she had to answer so; she did, "Hello?"

It was Mrs. Adams on the other end, "Mrs. Schultz?"

"Yes, this is she", Ruth responded.

"This is Mrs. Adams from the Welfare Department. I have some news for you. We have qualified you and your husband as foster parents. We'd like to know if you are ready as we have a child we could bring out yet today".

Ruth was still trying to get past the 'This is Mrs. Adams' comment and the rest of her statement was just starting to sink in. They did qualify and they wanted to bring out a child yet today? It felt like the world just stood still.

It really wasn't that long but it was long enough for Mrs. Adams to ask, "Are you still there Mrs. Schultz?"

"Oh, yes I am. Sorry, I just didn't realize you would be bringing a child out so quickly".

Mrs. Adams, realizing she had startled Ruth began to do some explaining, "You are correct. Normally, we would give our foster families a few days to prepare. But, a need arose for a young boy to have a foster home and I thought this might be a good fit for you. Plus, as you know, we have a shortage of homes right now, so we could use your help."

Ruth was trying to contain herself at the other end of the phone. All these things she was hearing were coming fast and furious. Today? Boy? Today? Boy? She just couldn't get past those two powerful words.

Finally, she pulled herself together and said, "Oh yes that would be great, when might you be coming out?"

"I could probably get there right after lunch around one o'clock," Mrs. Adams replied. "I do need to tell you that the boy we are bringing out has a few problems. He is currently with a foster family in St. Paul and we need to move him. It was only suppose to be temporary anyway. It isn't a good fit and he needs a change."

Ruth questioned, "I thought all foster homes were temporary?"

"We do have some who are only emergency homes where we place children for just a few days until we find a foster home where they can stay longer until permanent arrangements can be made. This was one of those homes."

Ruth heard what Mrs. Adams told her and it just took her by surprise. She didn't expect to get a child with problems. That had never occurred to her.

Mrs. Adams continued, "Sometimes it's good to put children who have issues in a country home, especially on a farm. It can help. I'm hoping this change to your home will help Billy."

Now Ruth heard his name for the first time. He must be William, she thought.

"How old is he", she asked.

Mrs. Adams responded with the facts, "He is ten but thinks he is at least 18. He lived with his father for the past 3 years after his mother died. Prior to that, he and his mother lived alone as his father moved out when Billy was three. His mother was an only child and her parents disowned her when she married and moved to Minnesota, as they did not approve of her husband, Billy's father. Since then Billy's grandfather died and his grandmother is older and in poor health living near Chicago, unable to take care of a young child. His father recently got sent to jail for a minimum of ten years for robbery. Billy has had to raise himself for the past 3 years, as his father was not too attentive to him. We were in the process of removing him from the home when his father got picked up for robbery. Billy is not very happy being in foster care. He seems to think he can take care of himself. He is very quite and somewhat isolated from others. I'm hoping that if he is in the right place he will come out of the shell he has built around him. His actions are probably a form of self-protection from the uncertainty he has lived for the past several years. I know this is a lot to ask of first time foster parents but we just don't have another place where we think Billy will be comfortable. Mrs. Schultz, you don't have to accept this assignment. Would you like to speak to your husband and give me a call back?"

Ruth thought for a few seconds thinking she knew she would need to speak with Samuel before making any commitments.

But, she did have some questions, "What is the long term plan for Billy and what if we take him and it doesn't work out?"

Mrs. Adams was careful in her response. Clearly, getting Billy a new home was crucial otherwise she would never bring him to a totally new foster family.

"Well, for some reason his father thought there would be money involved in raising Billy that's how we got involved. What we pay per month certainly wasn't as much as he expected. When he found out he seemed to want to just get rid of the responsibility, so it probably won't take too long for him to officially release custody to us. There weren't any other family members that stepped up so, the welfare department stepped in. Once his father signs away his parental rights Billy will be up for adoption and we'll look for a permanent family for him. It does become more difficult to find adoptive parents, as children get older. As to what happens if it doesn't work out for Billy with your family, we will look for another foster home, just as I am doing today. If there is one open we'll move him quickly. If not, we may need your patience until we do find one."

This was all so confusing to Ruth. Never did she think any of the children would have problems. And, although she knew they might be coming from families with issues, never did she imagine issues like this.

She finally did say, "I do need to speak with Samuel. I will go find him right away and call you back. Is that okay?"

"Certainly," Mrs. Adams agreed, "I will be in my office the rest of the morning. I was planning to pick up Billy around noon. However, if I don't have a place to take him I will stay in my office making calls until I find a place. I will wait for your call."

"Okay", Ruth said, "Good bye."

She hung up and a sense of fear came over her. How will she explain this to Samuel? He is going to be totally shocked, just a she was.

She knew she needed to get to Samuel right away. Heading outside she called for the girls, who were playing in the backyard with their dog Terry. She took them next door and asked Anna to watch them, as she needed to go out to the field and talk with Samuel. She then started her hike to where Samuel was working, with Terry at her feet. He was excited to take a run in the field. He ran ahead of her for a bit and stopped to look back to make certain she was still coming. He then started running ahead again. This continued the whole trip. It took her a while as the field was planted and she needed to walk between the rows and avoid stepping on the plants, which were just starting to break ground. Samuel could see her coming and was concerned something was wrong. He could see she was in a hurry. He got off his tractor and started to walk in her direction. Both of them were moving at a fast pace, without running, just long quick strides. When they finally caught up to each other they were both breathing hard from the exertion.

"What's wrong?" Samuel asked.

Ruth waited a few seconds taking a couple of extra breaths and then answered, "I got a call from Mrs. Adams. We were approved".

"That's great", Samuel said.

"Yes, it is but, there's something we didn't anticipate," She carefully added. Samuel was looking a little puzzled as Ruth continued, "She has a ten year old boy she would like to bring out this afternoon. Samuel, he has lots of problems. His mother died, his father just went to prison and his foster family said they couldn't keep him any longer. What should we do?"

Samuel was rubbing the back of his neck hanging his head down trying not to show his disappointment and trying to figure out what to do. Both of them were now looking at the ground wondering what to say.

Finally, the silence was broken as Samuel spoke. "Ruth, I can't say I'm not disappointed with this news. We were a little naïve in not asking more questions about the children or anticipating what might happen if we got into taking unwanted children. I'm trying to figure out why all of this seemed like the Lord was leading us to do this and now this. It's just so confusing."

As Samuel was speaking his words made Ruth think more clearly. That was it. The Lord was in charge and for some reason He has put Billy in front of them waiting to see if they too would reject him as he had been rejected by others. She started to share her thought with Samuel who was listening very intently.

"I just have to believe that the Lord is in charge. Maybe He is testing us. Or, maybe this is just what we are supposed to be doing. I know it won't be easy. It will be a challenge for our whole family. We can't let this hurt our girls. That we cannot do. But, I am willing to give it a try. Mrs. Adams said that if it didn't work out she would find another place for him. They will be trying to adopt him. He may not be with us long anyway. It will probably be temporary."

"Alright, I am willing to give it a try too. Let's go back to the house and give Mrs. Adams a call."

They both walked over to the tractor. Samuel would drive them home, as he didn't know if he would be back in the field again today. He had work he could be doing around home so he would be there when the child arrive. As they were driving home Ruth was sitting on the wheel cover sharing the footrest.

Samuel leaned over and said loudly, trying to speak loud enough over the tractors engine noise for her to hear, "does this boy have a name"?

Ruth said, "Billy, I'm assuming it is William".

Samuel nodded his head and they keep driving.

They hadn't gone very far and Samuel again leaned over speaking loud enough for Ruth to hear, "Does he have a last name?"

Ruth looked confused and then said, "I don't know, I forgot to ask."

Samuel again nodded as if to say it was okay, he was just curious.

⚜

Back at the house, Ruth went directly to the house, picked up the phone and dialed Mrs. Adams number. It was long distance so it took a while for the ring to go through.

Finally, she heard a voice say, "Mrs. Adams."

"Oh yes", Ruth said, "this is Ruth Schultz. My husband and I talked about Billy and we have decided we will take him. If you want to bring him out here today, that will be okay with us."

She could hear a deep sign of relief from Mrs. Adams who said, "That is great Mrs. Schultz. I will pick up Billy at noon and will be out to your farm around one o'clock. Will that be Okay?"

"Yes, that will be okay", Ruth said. They then said their good-byes and the call was over.

After hanging up the phone Ruth walked over to the kitchen table and sat down in one of the chairs. She could feel a tear rolling down her check. What were they doing was all she could think? Were they trying to replace one of the babies she miscarried? The first one would be nine by now. She had tried to deal with the three losses of babies and hoped this experience of being a foster parent wouldn't bring back all of the bad memories. Yet, she had a need she hadn't been able to fill, even though she had two wonderful children she loved so much.

Now, many thoughts were racing through her mind. She carried the first baby she miscarried the longest and when she lost it, although it was very, very tiny, it was already starting to form. It had tiny little hands and feet that were evidence that a life was forming and yet it wasn't meant to be for them. They knew it was a boy when she miscarried. As it happened at home they just didn't know what to do. It happened almost nine years ago yet the memory was vivid in her mind. After calling their doctor and telling him she miscarried, he gave them instructions that stunned them both. He told them to put the remains in a shoebox and bury it on their farm someplace. They were horrified yet they followed the doctor's advice. To this day it is difficult for her to walk beyond the barn into the open grove area where Samuel dug a small grave and placed the box, as instructed. Although he never spoke of it with her, she knew Samuel was as devastated as she was with the experience. It's hard to erase something so horrifying from your mind.

There wasn't a grave marker, as it wasn't considered an official burial. Samuel never told her the exact spot, as he didn't want her dwelling on it. The whole experience hurt Ruth deeply. It would have been comforting had the baby been born and they could have had a Christian funeral. Having a small coffin with flowers place on it, representing life would have brought the comfort she needed to bring closure. Had she been able to hold the baby and cuddle it, then it would have been easier to say goodbye. But that was not meant to be. She had only one vivid memory and that was the life she had felt inside of her. A life cut short.

Reverend Hadley had been a comfort to them both. He visited them often. He prayed with them and told them that they had a merciful God that would care for the child they lost. He sang with them their childhood favorite, "Jesus Loves Me" which took them back to the bible and its message of hope. They knew there was hope and they could look forward to happier days.

The other two miscarriages happened earlier in her pregnancy and she did make it to the hospital, going as soon as any discomfort started. The remains were disposed of by the hospital but she still always wondered what happened to them. She guessed it just wasn't for her to know and it was the Lord's way of protecting her from the anguish she endured from the first loss.

The fear of losing a baby made the birth of Martha and Rachel so joyous. Once Martha was born Ruth couldn't stop crying tears of joy. The Lord had blessed them with a child they could now raise to be a fine young lady. After losing another baby after Martha she couldn't even explain the emotion of being given Rachel. Ruth and Samuel had agreed to try one more time to see if they could have a boy. After losing the third baby the doctor told them Ruth shouldn't try to have more children. They both reluctantly agreed. Now, she needed to focus on her new responsibility of raising other people's children. She needed to get back to thinking about that and how they could do the best job possible in this new role.

She got up from her chair wiped the tears from her face and brushed her clothing as if to put things back in place to begin a new task. All that was left was for Samuel and Ruth to get things ready for their new young guest. Ruth had already gotten one of the extra bedrooms ready, one that faced the front of the house looking out to the road going by their farm.

Samuel was at a loss as to what he could do. He went out to the machine shed to work on some repairs that were waiting for him to find the time. He was working but his mind was also racing with so many thoughts about what it might be like with little Billy. When he started to make some noise from his repair work, his father showed up in the doorway.

"What you doing here? Did the tractor breakdown", his father asked?

"No, I'm here because we are getting a foster child this afternoon and I'm just staying around the house."

A long "Oh…", came out of his father's mouth. He then left to tell Anna the news, as he was certain she would want to know immediately.

He shared the news with Samuel's mother, not realizing the girls were in the other room and overheard what he was saying. It didn't take long and both of them were standing in the hallway looking at their grandparents.

Martha asked, "Can we go home now?"

"Yes, I think I saw your mother go back into the house after I heard the tractor come home." Anna said. "Be careful walking through the bushes, don't get scratched."

"We will", they both exclaimed.

They were now in a very big hurry to get home as they darted through the bushes that populated the ground between the two houses. As they reached the kitchen Ruth was just coming down the stairs with some things she had removed from the bedroom now set up for Billy.

"Mommy, are we getting a foster kid today?" Martha asked.

Ruth realized they had heard about the coming events of the day, "Yes, we are going to be getting a little boy this afternoon. He is ten years old and his name is Billy. You are going to have a lot of fun with him."

As you can imagine, the questions from the girls continued and Ruth did the best she could to answer them. Samuel worked swiftly at his repairs. Samuel's parents were busy talking about all of the possibilities with having another child on the property. Everyone was frazzled not knowing what to expect but anxious to find out.

CHAPTER 6

*I*t was about twenty minutes after one o'clock when Mrs. Adam's car turned into the driveway. She slowly drove down the drive and stopped next to the back steps that led to the back porch and kitchen entrance. You could see she was talking to someone whose head barely looked over the dash. It took a while before they finally opened the doors to the car. Mrs. Adams got out quickly but you could see the young boy on the passenger's side was moving slowly. He finally came around the front of the car. His head was cocked a little to one side. It was hard to tell if he had an attitude or if he was simply scared. Maybe it was a little of each Ruth thought.

The Schultzes waited until they got out of the car before coming outside. They were now coming down the back steps. Ruth had Rachel's hand and Samuel had Martha's. Anna and Gerhardt followed behind.

"Good afternoon", Samuel said.

Mrs. Adams responded with "Hello, thanks for letting us come. Sorry we are a little late. I guess I didn't anticipate how long a drive it is from St. Paul."

"No problem," Samuel responded.

Ruth's focus was totally on Billy, who was standing a bit behind Mrs. Adams. Although positioned behind Mrs. Adams he was still able to analyze the Schultz family. His face was a bit sullen as he eyed everyone standing in front of them.

Ruth looked around Mrs. Adams and said, "Hi Billy. Welcome to our home. We are so happy you are with us. Do you want to come in and take a look around?"

Billy looked up but kept his same expressionless look.

Mrs. Adams spoke saying, "This is Billy Spencer. Billy, this is Mr. and Mrs. Schultz, Martha, Rachel and Grandpa and Grandma Schultz. Why don't we go inside? Maybe I can sit and talk with Mr. and Mrs. Schultz while you look around."

They all headed toward the house. Samuel's parents decided to go home and said their good-byes. They'd stop over later and get caught up with what happened.

Once in the house Billy was shown around the main floor quickly by Samuel who walked him through the kitchen into the living room and dining room. All that was left was the bathroom, off the kitchen, the pantry and the stairway upstairs.

Ruth thought for a moment, when they were back in the kitchen, and said she would quickly take Billy upstairs and show him his room. She told Samuel to pour a cup of coffee for Mrs. Adams as it was already made on the stove.

She looked at Billy, who was still expressionless and said, "Billy, let's go upstairs and look at your room".

Billy all of sudden got a questioning look on his face.

Ruth said, "Is there something wrong"?

"I have never had a room of my own", Billy said very quietly.

"Oh", Ruth said, "Well, we have lots of bedrooms upstairs. The girls share a room because they are so young. When they get older they will also each have their own room. Let's go up and take a look".

Ruth glanced up for just a moment and caught the eyes of both Samuel and Mrs. Adams, who both were shaking their head slightly sideways as they were thinking, 'wow, someone hit a cord with this kid.'

By now Rachel and Martha heard about going upstairs and showing Billy his room and they were right there on Ruth's heals heading up the stairs. They actual slid by her and got ahead of both Ruth and Billy and were waiting for them when they got to the top of the stairs. They were anxious to show off their room, which overlooked the driveway and the backyard. To please them Ruth told Billy to come over to their room first and take a look. They showed off their room with their dolls, stuffed animals, pictures on the wall and anything else they could point out.

Ruth finally said, "Okay, that enough, let's take Billy to his room".

They all walked across the hall to the room just to the right as you come up the stairs.

Ruth walked in first and quickly turned as she got past the door to say, "Billy, this is your room. We haven't been using it so right now it just has a bed and dresser. We'll get some pictures on the wall when you decide what you want."

Billy quietly added, "I won't be here long enough to hang pictures".

That startled Ruth who had hoped the boy would be pleased to be with them and would want to stay. It was a strong reminder of how raising foster children is just a temporary assignment.

Billy took a quick look around the room and walked back to the door as if ready to leave. It was a little uncomfortable. They all headed downstairs back to the kitchen where Samuel and Mrs. Adams were chatting and sipping their cup of coffee. The girls asked Billy if he wanted to go to the dining room and play Tinker Toys with them. He shook his head 'no' and stood in place in the kitchen.

Mrs. Adams said, "I have to go now, Billy, let's get your things from the car".

She got up and headed toward the door. Billy just stood there until she asked him a second time to come along. He then slowly walked toward the door where she was waiting.

Samuel and Ruth were now looking at each other once Billy walked through the door.

"Oh my," Samuel said, "He really doesn't want to be here. This might be difficult. Maybe I'll go out to the car and see if he needs help carrying anything."

Samuel hurried outside so he'd be there if there was more than Billy could carry. When he got to the car he was surprised as Billy pulled a pillowcase out from the back seat and started walking back toward the house.

"Is there more?" Samuel asked.

"No", was Billy's short response as he walked back toward the house leaving both Samuel and Mrs. Adams behind.

Mrs. Adams turned to Samuel and said, "he has had a hard time. If things get too difficult give me a call. I will call you in a couple of days and see how things are going."

She then got in her car and drove ahead to the circle in the drive around the old windmill. After making the circle she drove back past Samuel and out the driveway to the highway waving as she left.

When Billy got back in the house, he didn't look at Ruth. He just walked right up the stairs to his room. He went in, dropped his pillowcase with his clothes on the bed and sat on the bed looking out the window. He could see across the highway. There were fields that seemed to go forever. Billy was not a happy kid. It didn't seem that anyone wanted him. His mother died and left him. His grandma hasn't bothered to even know him. His father is now giving him away. The foster family, where he stayed for a short while, asked Mrs. Adams to find another home for him. All he could think about is how long it will take this new family to put him out. He just needed to find a way out so he could just take care of himself. He did that for years when his father didn't come home at night and he got along okay. If he took to the road he'd find places to stay. He was young but he'd find a way to make money, he just knew he could. This foster home stuff was not going to work for him. These people are just in it for the money, just like his father was. Why should he help them get rich because of his misfortune?

Billy was determined to move on. He just needed to find the right time to do it. He also needed to find a way to get some money so he had a little to go on when he finally left. That would be his new mission, to get some money. In the meantime, he had to find a way to put up with these people. All their concern they were showing, it couldn't be real. They just wanted the money from the Welfare Department. He also couldn't wait too long before he made his move or his father would sign him over and some family might try to adopt him. He couldn't allow that. After all, he's ten and he can take care of himself. He kept reminding himself this as if he too might not believe it. Now he could hear someone coming up the stairs.

Soon he heard a voice, "Billy, can we talk?" It was Samuel.

Billy didn't respond. Samuel moved slowly toward Billy and stood next to him.

"Why don't you come with me and I'll show you around the farm? We have lots of animals. They'd love to meet you."

Billy looked up at him with a look that indicated he was too old to fall for that. The animals weren't waiting to meet him; they didn't even know he existed.

Samuel continued, now that he had Billy looking at him, "How about it, should we take a walk around outside?"

Billy reluctantly got up and started walking to the door. Samuel followed. Down the stairs they both went. Billy kept going until he got outside. There he stopped and waited for Samuel to pass him. Samuel first stopped at the machine shed and let Terry out. They locked him up so he wouldn't make a fuss when Mrs. Adams and Billy came. Terry was very happy to see someone. He did jump up on Billy and gave him one big lick across his face. It startled Billy who took a giant step backward almost falling down. He had never had a dog or even been around them much so this event was a surprise.

"Terry, stop", Samuel commanded.

Terry sat down. His tail was wagging vigorously, wanting to inspect this new visitor more. Terry loved all people, especially children. Billy leaned over putting his hand out cautiously toward Terry who reached his head toward Billy's hand and gave it a huge wet lick. Billy pulled his hand back, looked at it, and wiped it on his trousers. He then tried again and this time put his hand on Terry's head and started patting it. You could see that Terry loved this move and sat patiently until Billy stopped, at which time he looked up at Billy and gave a couple of quick barks, as if to say 'thank you', do it again. As Samuel watched Terry and Billy get acquainted he was thinking that maybe Terry could help get this kid to smile and open up a little. He certainly hoped that might happen.

They then headed to the chicken coop where Samuel pointed out all of the chickens, including the rooster and clucks that were sitting on eggs ready to be hatched. Then they headed to the barnyard where the cattle were eating hay in the fenced area outside the barn. Samuel told Billy these were the dairy cows that he milked twice a day in order to sell the milk. Billy was thinking to himself, 'so this is how farmers make money'. They sell eggs and milk. He wondered how much money they actually did make doing that.

Samuel said, "Look over there at the corner of the field at the crossroads. That's a schoolhouse where you will be going to school in the fall."

Billy looked up and sure enough there was a little white schoolhouse sitting on the edge of their property. How did he miss that when he drove by with Mrs. Adams? But, there it was in full view. All he thought about was how he wouldn't be going to school there; he'd be gone by fall. How foolish for Mr. Schultz to bring that up.

And, finally they reached the barn itself and they stepped in. Samuel gave Billy a complete tour of the barn from the milk house to the milking stalls, up to the hayloft and back down to the silo, which he opened and talked about how these would fill up during harvest. He seemed to be trying, in one full swoop, to inform Billy all at once about the farm. He showed him a couple of grain bins they had and explained more about the machine shed and all of the equipment inside. Billy tried hard not to show any excitement, even though there was some building inside of him. He had no idea of what to expect, as he had never been on a farm before in his life. This was a little exciting to him even though he was successful in his efforts not to show it. He certainly wasn't going to give in that quickly. He had no intentions of being here long so he was not going to get attached to any of these things he was being shown. Besides, they would take him away again anyway so, if he avoided attachments he would avoid any disappointments.

CHAPTER 7

*B*illy spent most of the day in his room looking out the window. He was thinking about what he would be doing if he were still with his mother. She had been sick for a long time so he did most of the work around the house. Even when he was six he was cooking for the both of them. He knew how to fry an egg, make a sandwich, heat up soup and he could even bake a cake, with his mother instructing him. Toward the end, when she was too sick to be out of bed, a neighbor lady, who was a good friend to his mother, came to help her. That's when Billy started to take care of himself.

When Billy turned seven she died. The neighbor wasn't a relative and didn't really want to take care of a young boy ended up calling the welfare department for help. Billy had been in 1st grade going into 2nd when he was given to his father. Since his father lived on the east side of town he had to change school. His whole life was turned upside down. His father hadn't even spent much time with him in the past so living with him was a huge change.

At first his father was interested in him. But, as time went on he lost interest. Mrs. Adams became part of his life stopping in frequently to check on him. Each time she stopped by and spoke with his father it turned into an argument. His father would yell at her saying he wasn't getting enough money to keep Billy and needed more. She would explain the rules and suggest that he look for a job and not try to live totally off what he got for Billy. That was meant to use for Billy's needs not the two of them as it was barely enough for just a child.

Finally, he said to her one day that they could take Billy because he was not good for him, it just cost him money and he needed to have his own life. He might as well put a knife through Billy's heart, as there was nothing else he could have said that would have hurt more. Mrs. Adams asked Billy's father to think about that when he wasn't angry.

It wasn't long after that when his father was picked up by the police, who took him away to jail. That's when Mrs. Adams did come and get Billy and put him in the foster home from where he just came. All those memories were much too fresh for Billy to handle yet; here was one more change in his life. What did he do that made everyone so unhappy with him? Why was this happening to him? If no one wanted him, he'd just take care of himself. He'd get away from all of these people who didn't want him anyway.

About that time he heard Ruth calling from the kitchen, "Billy, supper is ready, come done and eat please." He was a bit hungry, as he didn't eat since breakfast. Mrs. Adams had picked him up at noon and the foster home he came from hadn't served lunch yet. Mrs. Adams must have assumed he ate, as she didn't ask him whether he was hunger. He probably wouldn't have wanted to eat anyway. But, now he smelled something good coming from the kitchen so, he would give in and go eat. After all, he needed to eat until he was ready to leave.

When he got downstairs the table was set with a huge kettle placed in the middle of it. The girls were already seated both looking up at him when he reached the bottom of the stairs.

"You can sit here next to me", Martha shouted out pointing to the chair next to her.

Billy slowly walked toward the table and sat down in the chair she suggested. He then reached for a dinner roll on the plate in front of his place setting.

Ruth saw him take the roll and said, "Billy, we will wait for Mr. Schultz before we eat. Go ahead and leave the roll on your plate, we'll just wait. He should be here shortly."

Billy was a little embarrassed. This was the first thing he did since he got here and he was already doing it wrong. He now sat there with his perfected sullen look.

Rachel decided to add her own comment, "don't take bread, we wait for Daddy to eat.

Just then the door opened and in came Samuel. He headed right for the bathroom to clean up, a ritual he did before each meal. It didn't take long and he was at the table ready to say grace.

He greeted everyone when he sat down and said, "Let's fold our hands and say grace."

He looked at Billy, who didn't seem to know what that meant. Samuel took his hands apart and slowly joined his hands together, showing Billy what folding his hands meant. Billy followed suite and was then ready to pray.

They all bowed their heads, with the exception of Billy, who looked at each of them as they said the common table prayer together, "Come, Lord Jesus be our guest..."

That's all he heard. What were they saying? He had heard about Jesus, as his mother took him to Sunday School when he was Rachel and Martha's ages. He'd just been away from anything to do with church since he lived with his dad. Why were they inviting Jesus as their guest? He wasn't here. That didn't make sense to him. Just then he heard everyone say 'Amen' and the prayer was over.

Ruth asked him to hold up his plate and she would put the food on it. He complied and she put a scoop of beef stew right next to the roll he had already placed on his plate. It sure smelled good to him. He hadn't had anything smell so good for a long time. He put his plate down and just looked at it, while Ruth continued to serve everyone else.

Samuel started the conversation as Billy picked up his fork and began to eat, "Billy, maybe you'd like to get up early some day and join me in milking the cows. Now that it's summer vacation from school, you could do it in the morning or evening. You decide."

Billy hadn't thought about school as it had been out for a few weeks. He sure didn't plan to be there for the next school year, he'd probably be gone by then.

"What do you think?" Samuel asked again.

"I don't care", was Billy's response.

Samuel decided to leave well enough alone and not force the issue. When Billy was ready he'd ask to join him.

The meal was soon over and together they said the closing prayer "Oh give thanks unto to the Lord for He is good and his mercy endures forever. Amen."

Again Billy was listening and didn't understand what he heard. He thought to himself, 'how could they think the Lord was good when all these bad things were happening to him'. He didn't get these people. What kind of place is this?

Everyone, except Ruth, left the table and headed to the living room. Ruth started to clear the table. Billy stayed sitting at the table, not really knowing what he should do.

"Billy", Ruth said, "Why don't you join Samuel and the girls in the living room while I clean the table. We'll be watching a little television before bedtime."

He got up from his chair and headed toward the living room. Samuel and the girls were already seated on the couch. There was a lounge chair next to the couch and Billy sat there.

Martha quickly exclaimed, "That Mommy's chair".

"It's OK Samuel said, we'll get organized when Mommy gets here. In the meantime, he can sit there".

They all started watching TV. They didn't have a television for long. Sometimes it was hard to see all of the things going on. The picture was black and white and a little fuzzy but they loved the entertainment.

It took about fifteen minutes and Ruth came to the living room. Billy quickly got up to give her the chair. Samuel asked Martha to grab the pillow and sit on the floor in front of him. She quickly complied. He then picked up Rachel and put her on his lap. He patted the couch next to him and looked up at Billy who immediately came over and sat next to him. Billy wasn't used to having so many people together at one time. It was generally just his mom or his dad and most of the time just him. They didn't have a television and there wasn't much to do. This family sure seemed to be content with each other and seemed to like being together. He thought that was okay, as long as he was going to be here it might as well be pleasant. He longed to be loved in the way Martha and Rachel were. They belonged to the Schultzes and neither he nor anyone else could ever be the same to them. All he can do right now is just watch.

CHAPTER 8

The next few days passed quickly. Samuel and Ruth tried to make sure Billy felt welcome and they didn't want to press him on anything. They felt he needed time to adjust. He turned down Martha and Rachel enough that they figured out he didn't want to play with them. His friendship with Terry continued to grow. Each time he walked outside Terry ran to his side. It was the one thing he looked forward to each day. He did walk around the farm checking things out on his own. He found a special place in the grove behind the barn where no one seemed to go. He and Terry would wander off to this special place frequently. It was filled with trees and tall grass. It was overgrown and unkempt. He liked it as it was a little desolate and a good place to be alone.

Terry was always up for playing a game of catch with anything Billy would throw to him. It could be sticks or rocks, anything. He was very good at backing off as he caught a rock so as not to let it damage his teeth. It was an amazing thing to see him do.

One day, as the two of them were walking through the tall grass, Billy saw a garden snake and jumped backwards falling down. Terry instantly grabbed the snake in his mouth and shook it until it tore in two. Blood was flying all around and Billy had to crawl backwards on the ground to avoid getting splattered. After that, Billy would look for snakes and call Terry over when he saw them to see Terry attack. What a sight to behold, especially for a young boy looking for some adventure. They just had a lot of fun together.

Billy would also go to the grove to have a cry when he couldn't keep things bottled up any longer. He didn't want anyone to see him show his unhappiness, except for Terry. When the tears flowed down his face uncontrollably, Terry would sit close to him and lick his face and hands trying to console him. It often worked, as Billy's attention would move from his personal situation to his new loving friend. What was going to happen to him? The Schultz family was nice to him but he just didn't fit in. What could he do to stop thinking about all of this?

His other sanctuary was his room. He would close the door to keep the girls out and look out the window dreaming about where he would go when he finally ran away. The only thing he brought with him, other than his clothes, were a few magazines, which showed other places in the world. He would look at them for hours imagining being at those places having a good time. He loved using his imagination. He could be anything he wanted to be and do anything he wanted to do all he had to do was to imagine it. That was his great escape.

But, you can only escape for so long and then you have to face reality. Billy had been with the Schultzes only a few days. It was Saturday and he was told they would be driving over to see Ruth's brother, Albert Becker and his family. They lived about 8 miles north in the next township. Billy wasn't too excited about meeting relatives of the Schultzes but he didn't have much choice. Maybe it was good to get off this farm for a little while.

They got into the family car, which was a 1950 Chevy Coup. It was a nice car they had just purchased. It was used but it was new to them, the only thing Ruth and Samuel had purchased new since their marriage other than the farm. They hoped it would last a long, long time. Everyone was piled in, Samuel and Ruth in the front seat and the 3 kids in the back.

They took off out the driveway. At the end of the driveway they took a left. At the schoolhouse they took another left and now they were heading north. All Billy knew was this was the way back to St. Paul so he paid close attention in case he would be traveling there alone sometime when he left.

The trip was down a county road most of the way, which had curves with lots of hills and valleys. Trees covered both sides of the highway. In between the lakes and groves of trees there were farm fields, lots of them. Billy had never been outside of St. Paul his entire life. This country was pretty exciting to him as he took it all in during the trip.

He imagined himself running across the fields, with Terry behind him. They were on a grand safari chasing to get to a den of lions. He would capture them and bring them back to the Como Park Zoo, in St. Paul where he could see them whenever he wanted. He had a chance to go to that zoo once when he was much younger, his mother took him. He was in awe of all of the animals and wondered how they had all been caught. He'd love to take care of them, as he loved animals. That's why he loved Terry so much. As he looked back over the field he thought that maybe he'd also bring back a few monkeys and a tiger too. He could do anything.

Just then he heard Samuel put on his turning light and then they turned down a narrow driveway. He could see the house and barn in the distance. It was much bigger than the Schultz farm buildings and he thought they were big. These people must be very rich.

Ruth turned to Billy and said, "This is my brother's farm now but this is where I grew up. This whole area, as far as you can see belonged to my father. Look over there, across the field. That is the church where I was baptized and confirmed. My brother, Albert, has a large family but his kids are older. They probably will be out in the field working. We'll come back sometime and you can meet all of them."

Rachel had fallen asleep and was just waking up when she heard Ruth's voice. Martha was playing with her doll and wasn't paying much attention. But, Billy was wide eyed and hearing every word. This trip might turn out to be an adventure he hadn't expected. He saw some cattle in the field that were different than what the Schultzes had. The Schultz cows were black and white and these were brown and white. Should he ask? No, he didn't want to sound interested. They might think he was starting to like his stay with them. He'd just be quite and listen to all that was being said.

They were now at the house. Samuel drove around the circle in the drive, which went around a tree. Billy was thinking that all these farms have circles in their driveways. Maybe they didn't know how to back up so this way they never had to. Or maybe they just have so much land they needed to find a way to use it. Either way he thought it was quite convenient. The car stopped and everyone got out.

When Martha and Rachel saw two people coming down the back steps they took off running toward them. The two people turned out to be Albert and his wife Sarah who each picked up a child and gave them a big hug. Billy thought it sure looks like everyone in this family likes each other. That sure is different than what Billy was used to. Why couldn't his family have been more like these people? Maybe things could have been different for him.

As Billy, Samuel and Ruth got closer to the back door, where the others were, Ruth made the introductions. She introduced these people as Uncle Albert and Aunt Sarah. They weren't his aunt and uncle so it seemed strange to him. They both became very attentive to Billy welcoming him to their place and letting him know how happy they were that he came to visit them. Did they really mean it? Were they really happy he came or were they just saying that? They didn't have a reason to say that. Maybe they really meant it. Billy didn't get it. Why are all of these people so concerned about him? He just wasn't used to all of this attention. His father just left him alone and didn't really care much about what he did. He sort of liked all of this attention. He didn't know how to respond so he just looked at everyone with no response. Uncle Albert turned to Ruth raising his eyebrows when Billy didn't respond. Billy wondered what that meant.

Aunt Sarah told all of the children they could go out in the front yard and play. There was a huge sandbox and a couple of swings hanging from a couple trees out there. The girls ran to the two swings and began to swing back and forth the best they could without the benefit of someone pushing them. Billy decided to play in one corner of the sandbox making a castle with a mote around it. He imagined that dragon slayers lived inside protected from the dragons by the water surrounding the castle. At this very moment it appeared that all of the children were being just that, children. This was something not seen since Billy's arrival, all the children at play.

In the house Ruth's brother and sister-in-law were quizzing Samuel and Ruth about Billy. What was his background, why was he in the welfare system and how did they get picked to take him in? After hearing about his hardships they wanted to know if he was a problem. Did he misbehave? How was he with their two nieces? Were Samuel and Ruth worried about how he would be? The questions kept flowing and Ruth and Samuel answered each and every one of them.

Samuel began by saying," Billy had not been a problem. Yes, we do worry about him because he is just so quiet. We can't seem to reach him, although he has come out of his room and spends a little more time wandering around the farm."

Ruth added, "We just let him go as dealing with a kid like him is new to us. As long as he doesn't cause any trouble we're okay. Both of us keep an eye on where he is and what he is doing most of the time. Since it's been only a few days we hope in time he will become happier with us and being on the farm."

Albert asked, "Do you think you'll have him long? I hear that foster children either stay for years or just a few days. Do you know how long you might be taking in foster children?"

Ruth looked at Samuel before she spoke, "We haven't really thought about how long we might do this, and we are just taking it as it comes."

By now Sarah had lunch ready and the children were called in to eat. The Becker's had a very large table in their living room. You could seat at least a dozen people at their table. So, there was room for everyone. The lunch was made up of sausages, cheese, home made breads and lots of homemade relishes. Add to that a few different salads, bars and cookies and that very large table was full of food. Uncle Albert told everyone it was time to pray and everyone prayed together, just like at the Schultzes. Billy sat quietly as everyone said the prayer together. He was still trying to figure out why they were all so intent on praying but was also starting to feel a sense of belonging, which he couldn't quite explain.

After lunch Uncle Albert asked Samuel to come with him to see some of the new seeds he just took in as part of a test program he was involved in from the local seed company. He said he also was selling the corn seed for the seed company. What he had left probably wouldn't sell as most farmers had their fields planted. Samuel started to follow and then turned to invite Billy to join them. Billy got up from his chair and began to follow, wondering what this was all about.

Albert questioned Samuel as they walked, "How are you doing on that ten acre expansion you are working on?"

Samuel replied, "Well I have it all cleared and I have plowed it up once. I ran the disc over it and now I'm starting to pick rocks. We all know what a job that is but it actually wasn't too bad. It went as fast as the last acres I cleared last year."

That ended the conversation as Albert got the answer he was looking for and Samuel didn't have anything else to add.

They walked toward a building adjacent to the barn. It was a long narrow building with lots of doors along its length. Uncle Albert opened one of them in the middle. Inside were bags full of something lined up in a row. He heard Uncle Albert explain the differences between the different bags, which turned out to be seed corn. These bags were left from the planting already done. He told Samuel and Billy that as they drove out they could see the signs placed at the end of rows in his field to show the different corn that was planted. He would be testing the different kinds to see which one produced the best harvest in the fall. He was very proud of this venture.

Albert turned to Samuel and said, "If you get your ten acres ready to plant and its corn you decide to plant, I can make you a pretty good deal on the seed. What you see left probably won't sell and I'm not sure what the seed company will do with it. I will call them and see what kind of discount I can give. I think I remember them saying that after the normal planting season they would give up to 50% off. I'm not sure what they consider the regular planting season this year, but I'll check. Now if something happens to the field that would destroy the crops other farmers might look to replant and I'd have to discount them as well. You just let me know and I'll try and hold some for you."

Samuel didn't know what to say. Spending the amount of money he would need to spend to plant his field late in the season would be quite a risk. If he got a big discount, that would reduce the risk and increase his willingness to give it a try.

He finally spoke, "That would be very generous of you. I will need to make a decision quickly or it will be much too late to plant corn. After all, it should be knee high by the 4th of July and planting in June will be very late for that to happen. I will definitely call you as soon I know, thank you for the offer."

Albert was happy to help out, as he knew how hard it was for Samuel and Ruth to start a new farm. He thought a lot of his younger sister and remembered how hard she had worked on their family farm. If he could help them out he certainly wanted to do it.

It was quite warm in the building with all of the gunnysack bags of seed. Billy imagined this could be a fort and he could use the bags to surround him from the enemy. He would have imagined more except Uncle Albert interrupted saying he wanted them to come to the milk house and see some of his new equipment. They walked the short distance to the milk house, which was adjacent to the barn. It was filled with the biggest, most shiny big square things Billy had ever seen. Uncle Albert seemed very proud of all of this equipment.

He said, "These vats hold twice the milk as my previous ones and it keeps the milk fresh longer until the milk truck picks it up."

He explained a few more things about how it worked but that was beyond Billy's understanding. All he could think about was what a huge refrigerator these things looked like. In reality that's exactly what they were only a lot more. Billy wondered how expensive these must have been and how rich Uncle Albert must be.

It was time to go now and when the men were done with their tour Ruth and the girls were waiting at the car. Aunt Sarah has given them a couple plates of cookies to take home with them, which caught Billy's attention. He had eaten several of them at lunch and was pleased to hear they would be taking some home with them. Everyone said their good-byes and they were all invited to come back soon to visit again.

As they were ready to drive off Ruth opened her window and said, "I'll be stopping by to see Mom on Tuesday as we do our egg route. She's anxious to see Billy."

That caught Billy's attention. Now there was one more grandparent wanting to meet him. Why were they all so interested in him? He couldn't figure it out.

Ruth continued, "I'll see if she needs us to pick up any groceries while we're there so, you won't have to make a special trip for her this week."

Albert thanked her and they drove off. Billy was wondering what she meant by an egg route but, he knew he'd find out by Tuesday what that meant. Sometime, maybe he'd get the nerve to ask. Right now he didn't want to seem too interested so he'd find out by simply observing. His thought went back to the second grandmother he was yet to meet. He started to think it was too bad his own grandmother wasn't more interested in him. Here there were two that have already shown more interest in him in a short time than his did in his lifetime.

As they started to drive down the driveway on their way back home Billy wondered how far the Becker place was from St. Paul. He decided that the building with all of the seed sacks would be a good stopping off point for him when he decided to move on. It was warm and might be a good place to sleep, if he had to stay overnight on his journey. He'd have to keep that in mind as he made his great escape plans.

CHAPTER 9

*I*t was now Saturday evening, time for the family to gather in the living room for their evening time together either playing a game or watching television. However, this evening was different. Everyone was not going toward the living room, there were other things going on instead. Ruth, told the girls to go get their clean pajamas and she would fill the tub. She told Billy she had washed and hung his clothes out to dry earlier that day and he would find his folded on his bed. He hadn't noticed as he had gone right out to play with Terry when they got home from their visit with the Becker's. She told Billy he could use the tub when the girls were done with their bath. Although he didn't think he needed to take a bath he thought he'd better comply so he went upstairs to get his pajamas.

When he got to his room not only was there a pair of pajamas folded on his bed, all of his clothes, except the ones he was wearing, had been washed and folded as well. Plus, there was a new pair of trousers, a new shirt and some new underwear and socks there as well. Where did these come from? They weren't his; he never had anything so nice before. Why were these on his bed? Who put them there? He didn't know what to do or say so he just grabbed his clean pajamas and headed back downstairs.

When he got there Ruth was waiting and said, "Billy, did you find your new clothes?"

He reluctantly said, "Yes, Mrs. Schultz, those aren't mine, they must belong to someone else."

She responded, "They are yours Billy, I bought them for you when I went to town the other day for some groceries. I took a look at the clothes you brought with you and most of them are in need of repair and I thought you could use some new ones for church tomorrow."

"Church tomorrow" Billy asked?

"Yes, it is Sunday and we will be going to church and you will come with me and the girls to Sunday School. I teach 1st and 2nd grade. Mr. Stein teaches 5th and 6th, where you will attend. You will like him; he is a very nice man."

Billy was again quiet, this was a lot for him to absorb in a short time. He had been with the Schultz family less than a week and he had already experienced many more things than he could have imagined and he had a great imagination.

By now the girls were finished with their bath and calling for help to get dried off and dressed. Ruth got up and headed toward the bathroom. Billy was left standing by the kitchen table holding his pajamas as Samuel walked into the kitchen from the dining room to get a glass of water.

He saw Billy standing there looking confused and said, "Is everything okay Billy, are you waiting your turn for the tub?"

"Yeh", was Billy's simple response.

"Are you confused about something," Samuel added as he could see the look of confusion on Billy's face.

"I don't know", Billy volunteered, "I found a new shirt and trousers on my bed and Mrs. Schultz said it's for church and Sunday School tomorrow. I didn't do anything to get any new clothes."

"Billy, you don't have to earn new clothes, people can give things to you because they want to. It will feel real good going to church in your new clothes tomorrow. You just enjoy them, you deserve them."

Rachel was the first to charge out of the bathroom. Her hair was wet and she was full of excitement. She raced through the kitchen and into the living room through the dining room and back into the kitchen. Samuel caught her picking her up and giving her a big huge. Billy watched and wished someone had hugged him that way when he was small. He thought he was too old for that now but it sure looked good to him.

Martha came out a little more peacefully with Ruth right behind her. Ruth announced that as soon as their hair was dry it would be bedtime. Samuel said he would play a game of cards with them and maybe by then it would be bedtime.

In the meantime, Ruth said, "Billy there is water in the tub ready for you to take your bath. It's the water Martha and Rachel used. If you want to run a little more hot water to warm it up you certainly can, just don't run it over the tub."

Billy was surprised by all of this and gave Ruth a strange look, which prompted her to say, "Billy, we can't afford to heat a lot of hot water so we share the tub on Saturday nights. Next week, you get to use it first and the girls will use the water second, alright?"

"Oh, that's okay," Billy responded, "I just never had a bath in a tub before. We always used the kitchen sink and just washed off. When I was small my mother let me sit in the sink but when I got bigger I couldn't do that any more."

Ruth was now surprised by his response. She just assumed that everyone living in the big city had a tub but she now knew she was wrong. At that point Billy headed to the bathroom, with his pajamas to take his bath. It felt good to bathe in the warm water. Ruth reminded him to be certain to wash all over as his romps with Terry outside during the week probably made him very dirty. He decided he would do as she said and was very clean when he was done. He got out, dried off and put on his clean pajamas. He just stood there for a little bit and looked at the free standing tub with water that now looked a little discolored with a soapy ring around the edge. Things were sure different around here than he was used to and he sort of liked it.

When Billy exited the bathroom he saw Ruth sitting at the kitchen table reading through some material.

There was no sign of Samuel, Martha and Rachel. Ruth turned to Billy, who was walking toward the kitchen table and said, "Samuel is putting the girls to bed, which is where you should be going soon, as well."

As Billy approached the table he could see some pictures on the pages of the material Ruth was looking through. That intrigued him, as they weren't anything he recognized. He was always curious about far off places where he liked to picture himself.

He had a question that needed an answer, "What is this picture of?"

"It's the Sea of Galilee," Ruth answered, "Back in biblical times Jesus preached and met with his disciples around the Sea of Galilee. Tomorrow we're going to talk about one of his adventures in Sunday School."

"An adventure" Billy asked?

"Yes", Ruth replied, "Jesus had a lot of adventures. You'll have to wait for Sunday School to hear about it but you will see how exciting Jesus' life was".

Billy's face lit up as he was all for hearing about an adventure. Maybe Sunday School wouldn't be as boring as he thought. His life was so full of disappointments that he found great comfort in putting himself in other places in his imagination. He heard about Jesus before, when his mother took him to Sunday School. He was so small he really couldn't remember much about him, other than he was a good guy who people prayed to for help. He wasn't quite sure how Jesus helped people but he was told that He could and it always made him wonder. Maybe now he can find out the mystery regarding Jesus.

Ruth ran her hand through his hair to see how wet it was. It startled him because no one touched him with concern like she just did since his mother.

Ruth said, 'I think your hair is dry enough for you to go to bed. Do you want me to tuck you in?"

"No, I can do it myself." Billy responded.

"Okay," Ruth added, "I'll check on you when I come upstairs. Be sure you say your prayers when you get to bed."

⁓

It took about fifteen minutes and Ruth was on her way upstairs. She got to the top of the stairs and took a quick right into Billy's room. The light was on but he was fast asleep. The busy day and the warm bath brought sleep to Billy much quicker than he had expected.

His hands were still folded resting on his chest. Ruth couldn't help but smile knowing he was probably saying his prayers when he fell asleep. He certainly was a child in need and she was so happy that he so quickly found comfort in praying to Jesus.

Ruth turned off the light and went to the girl's room, across the hall, where she too found them fast asleep. Her heart was warmed seeing her little ones so content.

Entering her own bedroom she saw a similar sight. Samuel was already in bed, his eyes closed. She was careful to be quiet as she changed into her bedclothes. Then she turned off the light and slipped into bed. As she lay there she thought about how nice it was to have one more child in the house. She liked the extra activity and was feeling better about how Billy was doing. He seemed to be feeling more at ease. The conversation she just had with him, although short, was still a conversation where he actually participated. Things were looking up.

As one last thing before she fell asleep, she folded her hands and started a silent prayer.

"Lord, I thank you so much for this beautiful day. I always like going back to the old homestead. Thanks for letting Albert and Sarah take care of it so well. Help Samuel so he can feel good about his efforts on the farm. Keep Martha and Rachel the happy kids that they are. And, Lord, thank you for Billy, even though it could be a short stay. Help him to be a happy child. Keep us all safe through this night and make tomorrow a special day for everyone. In Jesus name I pray. Amen."

Now it was her turn to sleep. She rolled over to take a close look at Samuel. She thought about how fortunate she was to have him. He was so good to her and the girls and she was especially thankful for how he showed care and concern for Billy. He was good for Billy who hasn't had a good role model for a father in his life. Hopefully, Samuel's influence will be with him for a long time. That's as far as she got and her eyelids started to close and soon she too was off to a peaceful sleep.

CHAPTER 10

Samuel got up early the next morning. On Sunday's he tried to get an early start to get his milking done so they could get to church. On this morning his father joined him, which he did every Sunday in order to speed up the milking process.

As they were going through the motions Gerhardt was the first to speak saying, "Your momma had a tough night last night. I tink ve'll stay home dis morning from church. She said I should go but, I don't tink I should leave her alone dat long."

Samuel was done with his cow so; he got up and walked over to where his father was milking.

"Did she take her medicine when she got her spell?" he asked.

"Ya, it did help but, she still isn't feeling da best. I tink her heart is giving out as des spells are coming more often dan they used to. Da doctor says all he can do is to give her da medicine. I guess it's in da Lord's hands at dis point".

He looked up at Samuel and shrugged his shoulders. Samuel responded with a nervous smile and a slight nod of his head to show he understood and agreed with what his father was saying. Both of them went back to work, as there was no more to talk about. It was in the Lord's hands and they would have to wait and see how long she would be given to be with them.

When Samuel got back to the house, the children were all seated at the table eating. Sundays were busy getting everyone ready and it was okay for them to start without Samuel. He quickly cleaned up and sat down with them. They were almost done as he bowed his head and silently said his table prayer. Because everyone else was done, he also joined them in their prayer of thanks said at the end of the meal. This time Samuel noticed Billy mouthing the prayer along with everyone else. Billy had heard it enough times to know the words. Maybe sometime he would say it with them and actually speak the words, just not yet. No one pressured him to say it with them and he seemed happy for that. Samuel was pleased to see how quickly Billy picked up on it and that he was willing to participate, even if for now it was a silent version.

After they prayed Ruth told the girls that she laid out their clothes on their bed and they should go upstairs and start getting ready. She said she would join them shortly and help. She then turned to Billy and told him his clothes were in his closet and he too should go up and get dressed. As he got up from his chair she reminded him he should wear the new clothes she got him. He looked back toward her with a slight smile on his face and nodded his head yes and then headed up the stairs behind the girls.

Samuel said, "I would never have guessed, when he came to us, that he would make a change so quickly. He didn't even want to communicate when he arrived and now he is mouthing the words to the prayer. Did you see him do that"?

"Yes," Ruth responded, "He's been doing that since yesterday. I think he'll be joining us out loud soon. I am so proud of him. He is turning out to be a special little boy who has been through so much and yet has been able to avoid being bitter."

"We have a lot to be thankful for this morning when we go to church."

Ruth nodded in agreement and then asked, "How did milking go this morning? You got in rather fast."

"Papa joined me and that helped get things done quickly. He told me that Momma had a spell overnight and they won't be going to church this morning."

Samuel knew it must have been a bad spell as nothing short of something major would keep his parents away from church.

Ruth asked, "Do you think I should go over and check on her?"

"No", Samuel replied, "Papa said she took her medicine and was a bit better but apparently worn out".

"I worry about her," Ruth shared her concern.

"I know, so do I", Samuel added, "Papa and I agree there isn't anything we can do. We can only depend on the Lord to care for her. Her medicine won't cure her. It just helps relieve the chest pains and helps her rest more comfortably."

After they both nodded in agreement they got up from the table. Samuel went to the bathroom to shave and clean up a little more than he did earlier. Ruth headed upstairs to check on the children and get ready herself.

It didn't take Samuel long and he too was heading upstairs. He knew Ruth would have his clothes laid out for him so it wouldn't take him but a few minutes to get dressed. Hopefully everyone else would be ready when he got upstairs.

As he hit the top step he was met by Martha and Rachel who were on their way downstairs to sit quietly on the couch, as Ruth had instructed. Hopefully that would help them stay well kept in their Sunday clothes and freshly combed hair.

Samuel looked into Billy's room and saw him sitting on his bed reading one of his magazines. Billy appeared to be ready. He looked like a different boy with his new clothes. Samuel couldn't help but think what a nice young man Billy really was. He just needed a new look from the tattered clothes in which he had arrived at their home.

Samuel entered his bedroom and Ruth was just combing her hair. He loved how she looked when she was dressed in her Sunday best. She looked so sophisticated and she had such a delicate way about her making her a very special person. He never got tired of looking at her. She glanced up and smiled at him embarrassing him a little and forcing him to turn and start getting ready himself. It didn't take him long and he was ready too. They both started toward the door, as it was time to get on the road.

Samuel and Ruth stopped at Billy's room and saw him still reading his magazine.

Samuel said, "Okay Billy, it's time to go. Put away your magazines and come along."

Billy got up to put the magazines away. When he stood up he surely didn't look like the boy who came to them almost a week ago. He looked much different in his new clothes rather than his tattered and torn jeans and washed out shirt.

Billy put his magazines down and followed behind Ruth and Samuel, who had turned and started down the steps. Everyone was now ready for their weekly trip to church. This morning would be anything but routine, with the addition of Billy. The Schultz family had a lot to be thankful for on this Sunday.

When they got out to the car and everyone was in and settled for the short trip to church, they could see Grandpa Schultz hurrying through the bushes toward them. Samuel immediately got out of the car thinking something had happened and his father was coming to get them.

"What's wrong?" was Samuel's question.

"Nothing is wrong," his father responded as he reached the car, "I vant you to take my offering wit you and you put it in the collection plate".

"Okay" Samuel said, "How is Momma?"

"She is sleeping right now. I tink she is about the same. Wit some sleep I tink she will be better. Don't worry about dis; it will all be all right. You kids have a good morning."

Samuel got back in the car and waved good-bye to his father.

"Aren't Grandpa and Grandma coming with us", Martha asked?

"Not this morning" Samuel told her, "Grandma isn't felling well this morning and Grandpa needs to stay home and take care of her."

"Oh" was Martha's simple response.

They were used to Grandma Schultz being ill, it just hadn't happened on Sunday morning as she usually willed herself to be better so she could go to church. That just didn't happen on this particular Sunday. Samuel knew it must have been bothering both his parents tremendously to miss their day of worship in the Lord's house.

CHAPTER 11

*I*t was a beautiful day for their Sunday morning ride. Church was just on the other side of Greenville about 6 miles from their farm. It didn't take them long to get there. As they turned into the church parking lot everyone was getting a little excited. They all knew that Billy was something different in their family and it would draw a lot of attention.

Ruth turned to look at Billy whose eyes were looking all over taking in the sights. He was looking at the church buildings, the cemetery, the ball field, the parsonage and all of the people walking from their cars to the church. Because he was unfamiliar with going to church he wondered what the process would be.

Samuel parked the car and everyone got out. Ruth grabbed Rachel's hand so she wouldn't dart out in front of cars coming in. They walked across the parking lot toward the church. People whom they met on the way said good morning while they looked at Billy, but kept on going. They all knew the introductions would take place after church was over. As they entered the sanctuary and walked down the aisle toward the place they normally sit they got a lot of looks from those already seated. Ruth walked into their pew with Rachel still holding her hand. She walked Rachel into the pew ahead of her. Billy was right behind her with Samuel and Martha following. They were now seated and ready for the service to begin.

Billy was starting to feel uncomfortable as everyone who walked by, to sit in pews ahead of them, turned and seemed to stare at him. Ruth put her arm around his shoulder and pulled him close trying to assure him everything was all right. He looked up at her with a little fear in his face and gave her a nervous smile, which let her know he appreciated her concern.

Ruth then let go and reached for the hymnal in the pew rack in front of them. She opened it up and started showing Billy where the service would begin and where the first hymn was in the book. She pointed up to the front of the church where the hymns were listed on a big board hanging on the wall. She then pointed again to the number of the hymn in the book. Billy thought it was really nice that she was careful to do this all for him, as he would be lost otherwise. She did it all silently, just pointing and hoping Billy would understand.

At that moment everyone stood up including Samuel and Ruth. Samuel put his hand on Billy's shoulder and pushed him forward wanting him to stand, which he did. The service had begun and there was singing. Ruth pointed to the hymn in the book that Billy still had open in front of him. She ran her finger under the words. Billy read along as everyone in the church sang to the music.

What a friend we have in Jesus, were the first words of the song. As the song went on Billy heard a whole lot of things about turning everything over to Jesus. It's just like what he was told and what he had been doing in his prayers. He didn't know Jesus very well but he sure was willing to try and turn things over to him. It wasn't easy being alone and having a guy like Jesus to talk to seemed like a good idea.

Now Billy's mind was wandering as he thought more about the adventure Ruth told him about. Would it be as exciting as Ruth promised? He was lost in his imagination and didn't realize the whole congregation sat down again. Samuel now grabbed Billy's hand and gave him a little tug causing him to look up and see everyone sitting, which he then did as well.

It didn't take long and everyone stood again for the last song, after the pastor gave the benediction blessing to the whole congregation. After the song everyone sat down and the ushers moved to the front to usher out the parishioners. Billy couldn't help but wonder why they would stand and then sit so much during this church service. It was different but he thought, it was just their way.

Again, as people, pew by pew, got up and left down the center aisle, they all looked and smiled at Billy, sitting quietly between Samuel and Ruth. They were certainly all interested in him and seemed like they wanted the best for him with their caring looks and smiles.

Now it was time for the Schultz family to get up and leave, which they did. Samuel stood at the end of the pew and waited for Billy to pass as well as Ruth and Rachel. Martha stood by his side holding tightly to his hand walking out with him behind the other three. Ruth put her hand on Billy's shoulder guiding him toward the door where Pastor Hadley was greeting everyone leaving church.

As they reached the door Pastor Hadley grabbed Billy's hand and said, "So, you are Billy. I am so glad to finally meet you. I hope you are enjoying your time with the Schultz family, they are great people."

All Billy could do was smile. He didn't know what to say and, as was his practice, he kept quiet, as it is better to not say anything than to say the wrong thing.

Samuel caught up to Ruth and put his hand on Billy's other shoulder and said, "Billy has been great. We love having him around our place."

"Yes", Ruth added, "He's been very helpful. And, he's anxious to go to Sunday School this morning."

"Then we'd better let him go", Pastor Hadley suggested, "I hope you enjoy Sunday School this morning." Then he looked up to Samuel and Ruth and added, "This is a great thing you are doing. May the Lord bless your efforts."

As they walked down the front steps of the church Billy could see a crowd had gathered. People were chatting in small groups. Now eyes turned toward the Schultz family as they walked toward the crowd and focused on Billy making him a little uncomfortable. Several of the women walked toward them as they moved toward the crowd.

"Well, Ruth", said the first woman, "Introduce us to this nice looking young man."

"Yes, certainly," Ruth responded, "This is Billy Spencer. He is staying with us for a while. He is ten and anxious to get to Sunday School."

Billy was happy that Ruth said they needed to move on to Sunday School. He didn't like all of this attention he was getting.

Ruth turned to Samuel and said she was taking Martha and Billy and he should watch Rachel this morning. He nodded in agreement and picked up Rachel and told her to wave good-bye to the rest of them. She waved furiously and giggled as they walked out of sight across the parking lot.

Church was over and Billy was thinking that although he was happy that part of this Sunday experience was over he really did like the singing. If he was to stay here a while he might even try and sing along sometime. It didn't appear to him that anyone cared if the people next to them did a good job of it or not so maybe they wouldn't even notice if he tried to do it.

Now there was the experience he really was waiting for and it was to learn more about the adventures of this Jesus he'd been hearing about. He sure hoped it was as exciting as Ruth led him to believe it would be. He couldn't wait to see for himself.

CHAPTER 12

Sunday School took place in a building across the parking lot from the church. During the next hour Samuel would visit with the other men and women who were waiting for their children in Sunday School. They would talk about their farm work, the weather, politics and anything that came to mind while the young children played on the grass or on the swings next to the Education Building.

Sunday School started in first grade so Rachel wasn't old enough to attend. She would, at times, sit with Ruth as she taught her class. However, this morning Ruth decided, since she was taking Billy to his class and also getting Martha settled in, that it might be best if Rachel stayed with Samuel.

Ruth guided Billy and Martha to an open area in the middle of the classrooms where there would be an opening devotion, prayer and announcements. There she had the two children sit in chairs that were set up in a few rows. Other children came in and sat down as well. They were busy talking with each other and seemed uninterested in the new kid sitting there looking very nervous.

An older man went up front and told the children to settle down, as they were ready to begin.

He started by saying, "We have a new student this morning and his name is Billy Spencer."

That caught Billy off guard. He certainly didn't expect to be singled out like that. Now everyone was turning and looking right at him, just like in church.

The man continued, "Billy comes to us from St. Paul. He is staying with Mr. and Mrs. Schultz and we want to welcome him this morning. Billy, I am Mr. Stein and I will take you to your class when we are done with devotions. We hope you enjoy your time in our community and especially your time with us today."

That was a brief reminder to Billy that he really was only going to be here a short time. Temporary, that's what his visit would be. The timeline just hasn't been determined.

The introductions were now over and Mr. Stein asked the students to turn their attention back to the front. He asked them to look up to the chalkboard where there were some words written. Billy could see them but he didn't understand why they were there. Mr. Stein told the students that the words were from Matthew 4:19 and he asked all of them to read together as he pointed to the words.

They all joined in unison, "Follow me, and I will make you fishers of men." Billy was confused by these words. Mr. Stein asked if anyone had ever gone fishing. Almost everyone in the room raised their hand except Billy. He always wanted to go fishing but there wasn't anyone to take him. He thought to himself that someday he would sail off in a large boat and he would fish for huge fish that would fill his boat so it almost sank. When he got to shore everyone would applaud his wonderful fishing skills.

Mr. Stein continued, which interrupted Billy's daydreaming "Today, in class you will find out how Jesus recruited four of his disciples, or his followers, who were fishermen. When Jesus met them he told them that if they followed him he would make them fishers of men, just as we just read together. That meant he would teach them how to become teachers and preachers. Just like fishermen gathered the fish in their nets, they would gather in believers with the message of Jesus as their Savior. Jesus knew they understood how to fish so he used the comparison of fishermen catching fish in their nets to teachers gathering in believers.

Now Billy was getting more interested. He was starting to get curious about what Jesus would do next. He hoped the story didn't stop here but would go on.

Mr. Stein continued by saying, "I hope you enjoy the lesson today. Now let's pray together."

All of the children folded their hands and bowed their heads. Billy folded his hands but couldn't stop looking around the room at all of the children and teachers who were ready to participate in a prayer. He wondered how they got to a point where they always prayed and waited for Jesus to respond. He never saw any physical response from Jesus but he guessed they did or they couldn't possibly keep praying.

By this time Mr. Stein had begun the prayer, "Dear Jesus, we thank you for providing teachers and pastors who help us learn about you. Help us to be fishers of men and share how wonderful it is to believe in you. Make our time together special and let us leave excited to know you. And let us always want to be close to you. Help us to share with others so they too can feel how wonderful it is to know we are saved. In Jesus name we pray. Amen."

All of the children got up and headed to their classrooms. Mr. Stein looked at Billy and told him to come with him. They didn't have to go far. His classroom was only about six steps away making it a very short trip. All of the classrooms were in the same large room. They were just separated by dividers that kept them separate visually but you could hear everything going in the other classes.

Billy was very quite as he sat down at the table with the other students. There were ten students in his class made up of 4th, 5th and 6th grades. Mr. Stein sat him next to a couple other boys his age named James and John. None of the boys talked with each other, as they didn't seem to have anything in common to talk about. Mr. Stein had good intensions and it did help them all sit very well behaved throughout the entire class time.

As the story for the day began, Billy listened carefully. Mr. Stein was a great storyteller. Here is what he had to say.

"Jesus was walking by the Sea of Galilee where he ran into a couple of brothers named Simon and Andrew. He knew they were fishermen and that the boat he was standing next to was theirs. That's when he told them that if they followed Him, He would make them fishers of men. Then Jesus came upon two other brothers named James and John who were from a different family."

The two boys sitting next to Billy were amused by the coincidence in having the same names and started to giggle a little.

Mr. Stein smiled and continued, "He also asked these two brothers to follow Him. A crowd was now gathering and it got so crowded they couldn't move. Jesus told Simon to push his boat out into the water a ways and he would preach to the crowd from there. Simon agreed and Jesus got in the boat, along with his new found disciples and they pushed off."

Mr. Stein knew everyone was at the peak of their interest so he kept going, "After Jesus had spoken to the crowd of people he told the brothers to sail out into the deep part of the lake and throw down their nets. They told him they had already fished there and there were no fish but they would try it anyway. When they did that they filled their nets so full that they began to tear. Their boat was at a point of sinking and they had to call to other boats to help them. Jesus made that happen, it was a miracle and his new followers knew it. They were experienced fishermen and once they tried a spot and didn't catch anything that meant there just were no fish in that spot. Now they were fishing in the exact same spot where they tried and failed to catch any earlier. This time they caught an extreme amount of fish, which didn't make any sense at all. All they did was follow Jesus instructions and look what happened. It was a miracle or something that Jesus just made happen because he is the son of God and has almighty powers. That certainly was something only God could make happen."

Billy was in awe of what he was hearing. So, Jesus made the fish swim into their nets? How could he do that? Mr. Stein talked about Jesus being God. He wasn't really sure what that meant but clearly he must have great powers.

He tried to imagine what Jesus' life was like. He was able to walk all over the land and talk to people. He had a group of men that followed him and kept him company so he never got lonesome. He could go out on a boat whenever he wanted to and he loved to fish. That sounded really fun. What other adventures did Jesus have? Mrs. Schultz was right about the adventures he was hearing.

He really liked this Sunday School class. Mr. Stein told the fishing story, which is just what he was dreaming about earlier when he wanted to be a fisherman. Now he hears about Jesus doing exactly what he wants to do himself. What else should he know about Jesus that would be as interesting as this story he just heard?

Mr. Stein continued by asking the children to use the verse they learned this morning in their opening as their memory work for next week. He handed out a slip of paper with the verse on it, which Billy folded and put in his pocket. Then, Mr. Stein asked the students to recite their memory work for this week. Billy just sat and listened to each student recite. By the time all of the students recited Billy knew it well.

"For God so loved the world that He gave his only begotten son that whosoever believeth in him should not perish but have everlasting life. John 3:16".

The hour for Sunday School went by quickly. When everyone dispersed and headed back to the car Samuel and Rachel were waiting for them. Samuel looked at Billy and Martha and asked how Sunday School was.

Martha was quick in her response, "Daddy, they fish different than we do. They don't use worms or hooks or even throw out a line. They used nets."

"There are lots of different ways to fish, Martha", Samuel explained, "We use our way and people who fish for a living use nets so they can catch more fish faster. We don't need so many so we make it more fun by catching them one at a time."

"Oh," was Martha's response.

"What did you think Billy?" Samuel asked determined to hear from both of them.

Billy was engrossed in his thoughts of fishing on the Sea of Galilee when he realized Samuel was looking right at him waiting for an answer.

"Oh, I guess it was okay. I liked the part about Jesus making the fish swim into the nets."

Samuel seemed satisfied by his response as he looked across the top of the car at Ruth who was just opening the passenger door. They both just smiled.

Everyone was now in the car. Rachel was telling Ruth about her morning on the playground with the other small children. Martha continued with her comments on fishing and her version of what she heard about fishing.

Billy quietly was looking at the piece of paper he pulled from his trouser pocket. It had the memory work for two Sunday's on it. He was thinking about the words from John 3:16 and what they meant. So, God was a father who gave his son away? He was wondering if God gave Jesus away just like his own father gave him away, yet everyone thought Jesus' life was good. Jesus must have traveled the world; just like he was going to do. After all, being on his own would be better than staying in this part of the world where no one wanted him.

Was it a good thing that Jesus' father gave him away? Would it be the same for him? How could that be a good thing? It didn't feel good to him; in fact it hurt a great deal. He'd have to think more about this and maybe it will make more sense later. In the meantime, he kept thinking about the memory verses as he looked out the window taking in the sights as they drove home.

CHAPTER 13

When they got home from church Samuel let everyone off at the house and then drove the car to the shed. After closing the shed door he decided to take a detour and headed over to his parent's house. As he got closer he could see his mother out front with a bucket of water giving her newly planted flowers a drink.

He walked over to her and said, "Mom, how are you feeling? Do you think you should be out here lifting that bucket? Couldn't you let one of us do that for you?"

"Samuel, I feel much better now. I feel bad dat Papa and I didn't get to church this morning. How was it?" she asked.

"It was good; lots of people asked about you and sent their best wishes".

Samuel responded still looking her over carefully to see if he could see signs of weakness or other issues. She did seem okay. He wondered where his father was and then he saw him coming around the corner of the house having come out the back door.

His mother looked at his father while she spoke to Samuel speaking loud enough for both Samuel and his father to hear, "He insisted on making dinner. I think he is baking a chicken. He peeled the potatoes and took corn out of the freezer. I hope we don't eat blackened chicken and uncooked potatoes and corn."

You could see she wasn't happy that her Gerhardt wouldn't let her work in the kitchen to make dinner.

"I chased her out of da kitchen so she comes outside to work harder than she vould have in der. What are we to do wit her Samuel?"

Samuel looked at both of them and shook his head and said, "I'm not sure what to do with either of you. Why couldn't you wait and have dinner with us? Ruth is making it right now. In fact, I think she had it in the oven all morning, while we were at church, and it will be ready right away. You wouldn't have had to wait."

"My food will be yust fine" his father insisted, "You go and have lunch wit your family, we will be OK. And, oh yes, how did Billy do in church and Sunday School" his father asked?

Samuel started to smile and said, "I think he actually enjoyed Sunday School. He might have been a bit lost in church, which is understandable. But, he seemed to perk up after Sunday School. I really think he is a great kid. I can't believe he is as good as he is, knowing what he has gone through. I think he'll be alright."

"That's good," Anna commented.

"Ya, dat is good". Gerhardt also concurred.

Samuel headed back to his house where he found Ruth setting the table. She sent the children upstairs to change clothes so they could go out and play after dinner.

Samuel said, "I went over to see how Momma was doing. I found her outside watering her flowers. Papa was in the house making dinner. Neither of them were very happy with each other, I guess they are both back to normal."

"Oh my", Ruth said, "They are both stubborn Germans, which also makes them strong. I'm sure your mother isn't as good as she wants us to think. Yet, I'm happy she keeps going or she might just shrivel up and die. She's certainly a fighter.

At that moment all of the children came rushing down the stairs. Samuel and Ruth could never figure out how such small children could make so much noise going up or down the stairs. Now there was one more of them and they seemed to be racing, which even made it louder. It sounded to Samuel like a herd of elephants. It really wasn't a race for Rachel, who carefully hung on to the railing to avoid falling was far behind, as she giggled all the way down. She apparently got a head start, as she was halfway down when the other two passed her.

When Martha and Billy got to the bottom they didn't stop at the kitchen but ran right past it into the living room both falling on the couch giggling loudly as they each bragged about winning the race. Samuel thought as he witnesses this that it was the first time that Martha and Billy really interacted and it made him feel really good. It was turning out to be a great day, a day that the Lord has made.

Lunch was entertaining as the children continued to engage. Even Billy was keeping the conversation going as he told about the two boys named James and John and how two brothers appeared in the story with the same names. He thought that was great. Samuel said they must have been James Schmidt and John Hildebrandt. Ruth agreed. At that very moment they seemed like a very normal family. It certainly didn't seem like Billy had just arrived during the previous week, as he seemed to fit right in. Truth be known, he even showed a resemblance to the Schultzes with his blond hair and similar features. However, what really counted was his big heart and sensitivity that was certainly an exact match to both Samuel and Ruth and the girls.

All afternoon the children played outside. Samuel dug out an old rusty bicycle from the back of the shed and brought it out giving it to Billy. One would have thought he had been given the best gift of his life when Billy was handed the bike. He was a little shaky when he got on the first time but that didn't last long at all and he was riding up and down the driveway like a pro, with Terry running by his side. He soon made new paths around the shed and through the trees going toward his favorite place in the grove behind the barn. It was hard to drive once he got off the roadway but that didn't stop him. However, once he hit the tall grass it got caught in the spokes of the bicycle and it totally slowed him down. He had to finally get off and push it. He decided to turn around and go back as the driveway was a much better place to ride.

By this time, he could see both Martha and Rachel coming down the road in their tricycles to meet him. The bicycle was a boy's model and Martha was certainly not big enough to ride it so she didn't give Billy any grief for riding it. Once Billy got back on the bike and the girls turned their tricycles around the race began back to the house. It didn't seem like a contest except Billy's front wheel hit a rock in the road and it tipped him over. He caught himself before he hit the ground but it took him totally off the bike. By that time Martha caught up and rode right past him. He was now in a hurry and had to try several times to get back on before he could get going.

Rachel was trying hard to catch up but she had to be content to just keep peddling a bit behind. Billy pumped the pedals as fast as he could to catch up and hopefully go past Martha. The best he could do was to catch up just in time to have them both end up by the back steps together. Both of them started giggling uncontrollably as they thought about the event they both had just participated in. They were truly having fun together competing and although there were no winners there were also no losers in this game. Most important was they were having fun together and Billy was actually playing with the girls and enjoying it.

Back in the house Ruth was working on cutting out material to make a dress for Martha and Rachel on the kitchen table. Samuel had worked his way through the living room and had opened the front door going out to the porch. He settled in the rocking chair on the porch, where he lit his pipe and looked out at the cars on the highway going by the front yard.

He was just plain satisfied with his life right now. He had a wonderful wife, and two great children. He had his farm, even though there was still a struggle to own it. Yet, it was his struggle and he would enjoy the ride. He had his parents living right next door. They had a great church family and many wonderful neighbors. And, now he even had a boy living in his house, something he had hoped for a long, long time. Even though Billy's visit was temporary, at least he will have had the experience of having a son for a little while.

The two girls had gotten off their bikes and headed to the swings in the back yard. Billy sat on the back steps looking around the yard with Terry by his side. They had both been over every inch of the yard and beyond during his short stay with the Schultzes. He hated to admit it but he was enjoying his new life here. He just can't let himself get too attached so he won't be disappointed when he has to leave. While sitting there he put his hand in his pocket and came out with the piece of paper he got in Sunday School that morning. He forgot he put it in there when he got home from church after he changed his clothes. It made him think again about his mother dying and leaving him to his father who gave him away. He went from giggling with the girls to being sullen with the memory of his life. He got up from the steps and headed inside.

When he got into the kitchen he saw Ruth working at the kitchen table. She could see the unhappy look on his face and asked if everything was okay. She had heard the giggling a short while ago so she was rather surprised to see his face looking all sad and unhappy.

He shrugged his shoulder not saying a word. She was afraid he might be on his way up to his room where he would isolate himself for the rest of the day and didn't think that was a good idea. So, she told him that Samuel was out on the front porch and maybe he would like to join him. Billy hadn't been on the front porch so his curiosity took over and he headed toward the living room where the front door led to the porch.

He quietly stepped out onto the porch stopping right outside the doorway. There he saw Samuel just to the left of the doorway, rocking back and forth in the rocking chair while smoking his pipe. Billy saw another rocking chair just to the right of the doorway. He slowly walked over to it and sat down.

Samuel glanced up and could see Billy was very gloomy. He continued to rock, not saying a word, hoping that just being there would give Billy some comfort and maybe sometime he would tell him what bothered him. Billy started to rock as well although his feet didn't touch the ground so it was a little more difficult. He just looked forward not saying a word.

In what seemed like an eternity finally Billy broke the silence by saying, "Why did God give his Son, Jesus away?"

Samuel was startled by the question so he asked his own question back again, "Why are you asking?"

Billy took a little while but then he said, "This morning Mr. Stein had us say these words" and he pulled out the piece of paper and began to read, "God so loved the world that he gave his only begotten Son", that's where he stopped. "See he gave him away, just like my father did to me. Why do fathers do that?"

Now Samuel understood why Billy looked the way he did and he knew an immediate response was required as he said, "Fathers don't all give their sons away. Your father has some personal problems that he can't seem to overcome. Sometimes it's better if you don't live with someone who has his kind of problems. Also, the situation with God and his son Jesus was totally different. God loves everyone in the world and he knows that all of the bad things people do make it impossible for them to be saved. So, instead of making us pay the price for our bad deeds he decided to send his Son to suffer in our place. His gift was a sacrifice not a bad thing. It was the greatest gift God could give us."

Billy was listening intently. Samuel then added, "before Jesus paid the price for our sins he spent some time on this earth to go around preaching and teaching so the message of salvation would be here when he left this earth. Remember, just as you learned in Sunday School this morning. Then he ultimately suffered and was killed by hanging on the cross. However, there is a good ending to all of this. After he died he came back to life again in three days, which fulfilled God's promise to us many years before. So, you see, God's giving his son away was done in love. Your father did it for different reasons so you cannot compare the two."

Samuel could see that he had Billy's attention and that his words might be getting through this unhappy boy.

"In fact," Samuel continued, "I think God came to your rescue and got you out of a bad situation".

Billy was now in deep thought. Samuel didn't say any more, he didn't want to press Billy, as he knew he needed time to absorb this all. He was rather shocked that Billy had taken the words from John 3:16 and compared it to his own life. That isn't generally what he was used to. All he could think of was, leave it to a child to see into the words that we all take at face value.

Just then Billy spoke up, "So, if God rescued me, then he also put me here with you. Where do you think I'll be going from here?"

Samuel was shocked at that question because he really didn't have an answer yet he tried to give one by saying, "Well, there are some things that we just can't figure out and need to just wait for God to make the next move. It's called faith. We may not understand it but we accept it because God promised to send Jesus and God doesn't make mistakes. In fact, he already knows where you will be, he just hasn't told you yet."

This was all making Billy think very seriously about his whole situation. He started thinking about his plans to run away and start his own life. He was now wondering how that all fit into this situation. He needed to ask one more question before he put this to rest.

"What if we have plans that we think is what we should be doing? Do you think God put those plans in our head so we will make the next move?"

Samuel did his best to give a wise answer, "Billy, I think that God does work in many ways. He can make a suggestion by putting it into our minds or he can make it happen without any pre-knowledge on our part. It's really hard to understand. I just know that if God is involved and if we ask for his help, it will be a good thing. If we have something bad in mind then I seriously doubt it came from God. He gives us free will which means he let's us make up our own minds. He is always there for us when we mess up ready to help when we need it."

With that last piece of advice Samuel sat back in his chair and went back to puffing his pipe and watching the traffic, even though the cars were far and few between.

Billy also sat back in his chair. He was feeling much better about why God gave his Son away. He really didn't totally understand the concept of salvation but he knew it was a good thing God did for everyone. He also wasn't going to take the blame for his Dad giving him away. He agreed that his father had problems and it was best that he not live with him. Those years of being with him were not happy ones and he was happy it was over.

He still had a sad feeling deep down inside knowing that he didn't belong to anyone and he was basically on his own. It was nice here with the Schultzes but he also knew this was only temporary. It sure was nice being able to talk with Mr. and Mrs. Schultz. They weren't his parents but they were the next best thing right now.

CHAPTER 14

$\mathcal{M}$onday was washday and Ruth was up early gathering all of the dirty clothes from each bedroom. She rolled the wringer washer out of the storage room and hooked the hose up to the faucet in the washtub. This was a ritual she went through each week on this designated washday. She tried to get the washing done early in the day so the clothes would have time to dry on the line outside.

Ruth put in a load of clothes and started up the washing machine right after breakfast. As she washed the breakfast dishes she could hear the water swishing back and forth. She already sent the children outside to play, Samuel was back in the field and she was alone to do the laundry.

Just then the phone rang.

She picked it up and a voice said, "Mrs. Schultz?"

"Yes", Ruth responded.

"This is Mrs. Adams. I'm sorry to bother you but I have a couple of reasons for calling. I just wanted to check up on how things are going with Billy and I have a favor to ask."

Ruth didn't expect the call so she wasn't quite sure how to answer so she said, "Billy has been great. He has his ups and downs but all in all I think he's enjoying himself. What is the favor you need?"

There was a little hesitation on the phone and then, all at once, Mrs. Adams charged forward with her request for a favor, "I need to ask you if you would consider taking in a newborn baby for a few days.

It came prematurely over the weekend and the adoptive parents are on a vacation, out of town and can't get back here for a few days, maybe a week. I know this is sudden but I don't have any other place to take the baby. All of my foster parents are full up right now. Would you consider doing this?"

Ruth was so taken back by this request it left her speechless. Some time past and she just couldn't find the words to respond.

"Mrs. Schultz, are you still there," came the voice on the phone.

Ruth tried to gather her thoughts and respond but couldn't get the words out.

"Would you like to talk with your husband and call me back? If you can take the child I would bring him out yet today," Mrs. Adams inserted while she waited for Ruth to speak.

Ruth finally pulled herself together and spoke, "Yes, I do need to speak with Samuel. This is quite sudden. So, you say it will only be for a few days?"

"Yes", Mrs. Adams said, "only a few days until the new parents can get back into town,"

"Okay, I will speak with Samuel and call you back within the hour."

They said their good-byes and now Ruth sat down in the chair next to the kitchen table to gather her thoughts about what just happened. She wondered how this was all happening to them so quickly after they agreed to become foster parents. It was only going to be just a few days and then they would be back to just Billy. Although, who knows how long Billy will be with them?

It seemed like a dream that she had dreamed before as Ruth went next door and asked her mother-in-law if she felt well enough to watch the children. Anna assured her she could watch the children. Ruth told her the children were in the backyard and she would tell them to stay there. As she started down the path back home, Anna followed right behind. As she came close to the children she told them to stay in the yard where their grandma could see them.

"Where are you going?" was the response by the children almost in unison. Even Billy chimed in, as he too was always up for an adventure, if Ruth would let him tag along.

"I need to go to the field and talk with Daddy," she told them.

"Can I come, Mommy?" Rachel was the first to speak.

"Not this time. I won't be long," Ruth said as she began to walk away toward the field.

She headed out toward the north ten acres to find Samuel. This time she wasn't in quite as big a hurry as so much was going through her mind. They hadn't planned on taking in a baby this soon. She purposely stayed away from discussion about a baby, as she didn't want any reminders of the ones she lost. It would only be a few days. She could deal with that. This poor baby needed her until his new parents arrived. Why did they leave town so close to its birth date? Yes, it was premature but they should have anticipated that possibility. Babies can come early. What did she want to do? If she said 'no' where would Mrs. Adams take the poor baby? Maybe it would go to someone who didn't care about him and that would be terrible for that small thing. It wasn't looking like she had a way out of this.

She was walking slower and slower and she finally realized it so, she picked up the pace. The corn had popped up out of the ground so she also was especially careful to walk between the rows to avoid stepping on any fresh plants. She could see Samuel in the distance. He was walking across his new field picking rocks and throwing them on the wagon he parked close by behind the tractor. He worked so hard.

Then her thoughts went right back to the baby. Would Samuel see this the same way and be willing to take this challenge in front of them? They were just getting used to having Billy with them and so quickly another child. Then it hit her like a ton of bricks. This baby was a boy. How is it that each child Mrs. Adams wants to bring to them is a boy? She didn't even ask if the baby had a name. Things were happening way too quickly for her.

By now Samuel saw her coming and waved. This time he didn't come out to meet her, as her stride was more relaxed than her last trip so, he didn't think there was a crisis to which he needed to respond. He did wonder what Ruth was coming out to tell him but he'd wait for her to get there. He could throw a few more rocks in the wagon by the time she got there. He was almost done and if he stuck with it he might finish today and then he could still plant the new field. He was thinking about Albert's offer to give him some corn at a reduced rate. He just needs to see how much he collects on the egg route tomorrow and then he would decide what he could buy.

He looked up again and Ruth was just a few yards away. He stood up and brushed off his gloves and clothes trying to look a little less dirty from his dirty work.

"What's up?" he asked as she gave him a nervous smile stopping right in front of him.

"I just got a call, Samuel, from Mrs. Adams. She asked if we would consider taking in another foster child for a short time.

"You don't say," was Samuel's immediate response.

"It's a baby who was born prematurely over the weekend and the adoptive parents are out of town for up to a week and can't pick it up. She said she doesn't have any place to take him."

Ruth blurted it all out before Samuel could speak. By now he was looking a little puzzled as he too hadn't expected another foster child in their home so quickly.

Ruth added, "She wants to bring the baby out today. I have mixed feelings about taking a baby but Mrs. Adams sounded desperate."

Samuel turned around, walked over to the wagon and sat down on an open area near the edge. He hung his head down and remained silent for what seemed like an eternity, although it was probably just a minute. Ruth walked over to the wagon and put her hand on Samuels, which he was resting by his side. When she did that he started to speak.

"I never knew that we would be given so many challenges as a couple. I wondered when we lost our babies whether the Lord wanted us to have children and then he followed up with the girls. I could hardly bear losing the last one and was convinced he just didn't want us to have any sons. But now, we are being given a different test. Are we are being tested by having these foster children come to us as only boys, knowing they will only be with us temporarily? I know this is only the second one but is it just coincidence that it too is a boy? I'm having trouble figuring it all out."

Ruth listened and seemed to be trying to figure out where Samuel was going with his comment. Samuel could see from the look on her face that she was determined to get an answer from him. Before he could say another word she pressed on.

"So, do you think I should tell Mrs. Adams we have our hands full with Billy and now isn't a good time as we aren't ready for more."

Without hesitation Samuel responded, "Oh no, that isn't what I meant at all. We need to do this. The Lord has put these challenges in front of us and we can't walk away. Didn't you say it would be for just a week?"

Ruth gave a nod in agreement while he continued, "Well, I think we can do that. It will only be temporary."

"Okay," Ruth said, "I'll call Mrs. Adams and tell her. Then I'll dig out our old crib and get it ready. Maybe we can just put the crib in our room instead of making the baby sleep alone in the vacant bedroom. It's just for a week and it is just a little premature and might need a little more attention."

Samuel nodded and they both got up and started off in different directions. He watched as Ruth walked back toward the house with a little extra lift to each step. He started back to picking rocks and then stopped and looked at Ruth again. He too had a little more energy but just needed to watch Ruth wondering if this experience would be good or bad for her. At least it would only be a week. It certainly couldn't have a negative affect in such short time.

He then decided that he needed to go back to the house and help get things ready so Ruth didn't have to go up to the attic and uncover the crib and also clean it up alone. He could do that while she got other things ready, like bottles, diapers and anything else a baby might need. Besides, he wouldn't be able to keep his mind on his work after this exciting news anyway.

He started the tractor, got on it and started toward the road. It's too bad he didn't think of this quicker and then Ruth could have driven back with him rather than having to walk. She'd understand and probably appreciate his help.

He had to take the long way home, which was out the backside of their property and onto the road all around the perimeter of their land. He could no longer drive over the field now that the corn had started to come up. He enjoyed driving the tractor and doing it on the road was a joyful departure from the bumpy field.

Samuel drove in the driveway just as Ruth was walking to the house. She was surprised to see him, as she knew he had a little more work to do before he would call it a day. The only thing she could think of was that he was as excited about their new arrival as she was. Samuel drove past her with a smile on his face giving her a bit of a salute as he passed. She just smiled and waved back with a huge grin knowing they both were excited.

She walked over to where the children were playing and Anna was sitting in one of the lawn chairs. After watching what they were doing for a short time, she finally spoke to all of them.

"I got a call from Mrs. Adams this morning. After I call her back she will be coming out this afternoon. I know we didn't expect her back so soon but this is a special trip. Try and stay clean so you don't have to change clothes before she gets here."

Anna got up and followed Ruth to the house.

"What does Mrs. Adams want?" Anna asked.

"Oh, I forgot to tell the children," Ruth seemed distracted as she walked up the back steps. "She is bringing a baby for us to take care of for about a week until the adoptive parents can get here from out of town."

Anna was both surprised and concerned when she said, "Dat seems a little soon. You just started taking in children and now a second one is coming so soon? Can you handle taking care of a baby wit all of your work around here?"

Ruth didn't want to let logic make this decision as she already had her mind made up that she would be able to do it. Yet, she knew she owed Anna an answer.

Without missing a step or looking back she responded saying, "We'll manage. After all, it's only temporary".

She entered the porch door heading to the phone to call Mrs. Adams without looking back at Anna. She didn't want to take the chance they would talk more and that she'd be talked out of taking this newborn. Just an hour ago she wasn't certain about doing this and now she really wanted it.

The phone call was quick and to the point. Ruth said she and Samuel agreed to help out and take the baby. Mrs. Adams thanked her and said she'd be out around three o'clock. She asked Ruth if she needed to bring baby supplies. Ruth assured her that they had many things left from when Rachel was a baby and they probably had what they needed for now. The call was then over and both women ended the call feeling good, knowing that things were going as they wanted them to go. This was a good day.

CHAPTER 15

Ruth's words about Mrs. Adams making a surprise visit sent chills up and down Billy's spine. He was sure that meant Mrs. Adams was coming to take him away. He didn't know what to do, this couldn't be happening to him so soon after he got here. Why? He didn't do anything wrong. Was someone trying to adopt him? He didn't want to be adopted, not now when he just started to feel more comfortable right here with the Schultzes. Did he have to pack and get out before Mrs. Adams got there? This was so sudden he just couldn't believe it.

He had to get away and think. He took off to his favorite place in the grove of trees behind the barn. As usual, Terry was by his side. Now he was sitting next to a tree on the ground in the tall grass. His knees were bent and he held on to them with his hands. This wasn't new as he sat there many time before so the grass was pressed down. There was more than enough room for him and Terry to sit without the grass poking them. The grass actually served as a carpet protecting them from the ground.

He sat there for a while not knowing what to do. He was overwhelmed with a feeling of sadness. Tears started to run down his cheeks and he couldn't stop them. In fact, it didn't take long and he put his head on his knees and sobbed uncontrollably. Terry sat closer and closer as he watched Billy sob. He tried to rub his nose under Billy's arm to make him lift up his head but it didn't work as Billy just kept crying and hanging on tightly to his knees. Billy knew they were in a safe place that no one ever visited. He never understood why but he was happy to have a place of his own.

After about five minutes he finally lifted his head and the sobbing started to subside. The tears were still running down his face as he started to rub them away with his hands. He then rubbed his eyes as he tried to clear them so he could see better from the flood of tears that filled them. He was just so sad that nothing could console him.

The unanswered questions in his life all came back again. Why was he so alone? Why did he lose his mother? Why did his father and his grandmother not want him? What did he do that was so wrong to deserve this in his life?

He was trying to reason it all out and nothing seemed to work. And then he started to think about what he heard in Sunday School. Why didn't Jesus come and help him? He really needed some help. He prayed at night, like Mrs. Schultz told him to do. Didn't he say the right things? He was new at this; couldn't Jesus understand that and give him a break?

Then out of total frustration he started to speak to Jesus. "Jesus, I've been told that if I ask for your help you will give it to me. I really need your help now. Mrs. Adams is coming to get me and I don't know where she is taking me. I don't want to go. I like it here, why can't I stay here? Why does everything get taken away from me? If there is something you can do to help would you do it now? I don't have much time before Mrs. Adams will be coming. If Mrs. Schultz called her I'm sure it won't take her more than an hour or two and then I'll be gone. Please help me?"

With that he put his head on his knees again and just rested for a little while without doing or thinking anything. If Jesus was going to help him it needed to be right now, or at least before Mrs. Adams arrived. It was hard to trust when he has experienced so many disappointments in his life.

He felt he needed to do something. Maybe he should go get his stuff and head out before Mrs. Adams got there. Maybe now was the time to take that journey he'd been thinking about for sometime. He didn't have any money but maybe he could find a job somewhere, after he got away.

He decided to take action. As he got up he patted Terry on the head, as he knew he couldn't take him along and he'd have to leave him behind. Then he knelt down and gave Terry a huge hug and buried his head in Terry's neck and hung on for a while. Terry just sat there not want Billy to quit. Billy finally did let go, got up and started back toward the barn on his way to the house with Terry at his heels.

Samuel was up in the attic moving boxes in order to get at the crib they had placed there a couple years ago. He finally cleared a path and he reached his target. After unloading some small items from the crib he picked it up and took it to the attic stairs. The stairs were steep so he was very careful as he headed down holding onto the crib tightly. He reached the second floor and put down the crib.

When he finally got the crib into the light he saw that one side had a crack in it. He knew he needed to fix that so it would be totally safe for the baby. Even though a newborn wasn't likely to move around too much, he wanted to be sure the crib was safe. He picked up the crib and headed down the stairs to the first floor. When he got to the bottom, Ruth was there cleaning bottles at the sink.

"Where are you going with the crib?" was her question to Samuel.

"The crib has a crack on one side. I'm taking it out to the shed and fixing it. I'll bring it back so we can clean it up after I get it fixed." He stood there for a while to give more details. "I won't be long. I left the mattress in the hallway upstairs. It's a good thing we wrapped it up, as it is really dusty in the attic. You'll want to check it out. Maybe we should take it outside and let it air out a little before we put it in the crib."

"That sounds like a good idea," Ruth said in agreement, "I'll go upstairs in a bit and take it out of the wrapping and see what it looks like."

At that Samuel headed out the back door, through the porch and out the porch door. As he headed toward the shed he passed Billy, who was on his way to the house. Samuel was preoccupied and didn't notice Billy's red eyes and dirty cheeks from rubbing the tears with his dirty hands. You could see how the tears ran down his cheeks across his dirty face. Samuel was focused on carrying the crib to the shed and part of the crib blocked his view. They passed each other in silence and kept moving.

Billy entered the kitchen, as Ruth was finishing up washing the bottles and all of the paraphernalia that went with them. She was putting the towel on the rack to dry as Billy walked through and started up the stairway. Again, nothing was said by either of these two preoccupied people. This was the first time that Billy practically ran up the steps as he was on a mission to gather his things and find a way to get out unnoticed.

On his way back from the grove he decided he would fill the pillowcase he had his things packed in when he came and drop it out the window. He would pick it up when he went outside to leave. He'd have to be careful that Grandpa and Grandma Schultz didn't see him, as his window was on their side of the house.

When he got upstairs and into his room he looked around and he remembered he really didn't have too many things to pack. His whole life could be packed into a pillowcase. He went to his closet and started to look for his pillowcase. At first he couldn't find it and then he noticed it on the closet shelf. It had been washed and folded neatly. He then remembered how Mrs. Schultz had washed and dried all of his clothing when he came. Then he saw the new trousers and shirt hanging there in front of him. It was the nicest gift anyone had given him because Mrs. Schultz noticed him and got him something he really needed. He hadn't felt that special for a long time. He would miss that attention.

When he got his clothes stuffed into the pillowcase he walked over to the dresser and opened the top drawer where he kept his magazines. He pulled them out and took them over to the bed, where he had the half-packed pillowcase. As he started to put each magazine on top of his clothes he couldn't help but look at each one and remember the dreams he had within their pages.

Billy was about halfway done when he felt the presence of someone else. When he looked up he saw Mrs. Schultz standing in his doorway. It caught him totally off guard.

"What are you doing Bill?" Ruth said with a great deal of compassion in her voice. "Are you going somewhere?"

Billy was speechless, as he never expected to get caught. All of a sudden he felt the tears returning and slowly running down his face. Ruth had moved closer and actually sat on the bed next to his pillowcase and stack of magazines. She was now close enough to see his emotions ready to burst. Since Billy didn't dare speak for fear of bursting into tears Ruth spoke again.

"I can see something has you upset. Do you want to tell me about it?" Billy shook his head no and looked down at the floor hoping to hide the tears that were now dropping to the floor.

Ruth felt tears welling up in her eyes as well as she watched how sad this little boy was standing in front of her. She just couldn't figure out what was going on here with Billy but could see it was bothering him immensely. All she could do was to grab him and hold him tightly, which she did. When she did that, Billy broke down. He grabbed her around the neck and sobbed again uncontrollably. She started rubbing his back hoping to soothe the pain of whatever was upsetting him.

"Oh Billy," she said tenderly, "What has you so upset? Did something happen that hurt you?"

Billy just kept hanging on to her. He so needed someone to hold him. He was now that little ten-year-old boy, not the young man he always tries to be.

After a little time past the sobbing subsided but he was still burying his head in the nap of Ruth's neck. For the first time in a long time he felt secure with Ruth holding him. He didn't want her to let go. Finally, when she thought he was done sobbing she let up on her tight grip, still leaving her arms around his back and waste.

Billy started to let go slightly. When he did, Ruth pushed him back slowly until he lifted his head back and they were now face to face. First she reached up and wiped the tears from her own face with one hand while still hanging on to Billy's waste keeping him close. Then she reached into the pocket of her apron and pulled out a handkerchief that she used to wipe Billy's cheeks. She could now see how his face had been rubbed with his hands and how streaks of tears had run down his face leaving a residue that gave it all away. She was so careful and so loving that it truly showed how much she cared for this child. All she wanted to do was ease the pain by showing she cared.

Ruth spoke asking her question again, "Now tell me what is bothering you, Billy."

After careful hesitation Billy reluctantly replied, "Why is Mrs. Adams coming to get me? Did I do something wrong? Is someone trying to adopt me? I don't want to be adopted and go with some strangers."

Ruth immediately figured out that Billy only heard that Mrs. Adams was coming and never heard about the baby she was bringing. That was like a knife in her heart as she realized she had caused his pain by not telling the children everything. She was so focused on the baby that she forgot about the children and how they felt about this. With little information Billy came to his own conclusion.

Ruth pulled Billy close to her again and with his head resting on her shoulder she said, "I am so sorry. I didn't tell everything Mrs. Adams called about. She isn't coming to get you. She is bringing out a baby for us to take care of for a short time until his adoptive parents can get here. This isn't about you, although I'm certain she will want to visit with you when she comes. You can stay here in our home until you are ready to leave."

She then pushed him back up again and looked right into his eyes and said," We love you Billy Spencer and although it's just been a short time you have been with us, we enjoy you being here and hope you enjoy it as well."

Billy was stunned as he spoke, "Mrs. Adams is bringing out a baby? And, I can still stay?"

"Yes," Ruth replied emphatically as she repeated it more clearly. "You can stay. I don't know what the future holds and if you will ever have adoptive parents. But, until that happens you are more than welcome in our home, and don't you ever forget that."

A huge sigh of relieve came over Billy's whole body as he relaxed and managed to show a little grin. Ruth then needed to ask one more last thing,

"So are you okay now? Can I help you unpack or are you okay doing it yourself?"

"I can do it, I don't have too much anyway," He responded.

Ruth then looked up and took a glance around his room seeing how bare the walls were and not a thing on the top of the dresser to even show that someone lived there.

"Billy," she said, still looking around. "I promised that you could do some decorating when you came and we haven't done that yet. We are going to find a time and go up to the attic and see if there is anything that you might want for your walls and things you might want to put on your dresser to spruce up this room a bit. Will that be alright with you?"

"Oh yes, I would really like that, Mrs. Schultz," Billy said with a little excitement in his voice. "I've never had my own room so I won't know what to put up."

"We'll find something, I'm certain," she assured him. "We have lots of things up there that we took down and put there when we moved in and replaced with our own decorations. There are also many things the former owners left that we have never had the chance to look through. I just know you will find something from that whole menagerie of things in the attic. Let's get through with Mrs. Adams' visit and then we'll get up there and look around."

Ruth now got up and walked to the door. She then paused, turned partway and smiled at Billy before she moved into the hallway over to the crib mattress. As she started unwrapping it she couldn't stop thinking about what just happened. This little boy was so upset. She decided she needs to be more aware of his sensitivity in the future. He needed much more attention than she thought. His independent exterior must be a camouflage for a very tender interior.

Billy stood at the side of his bed for a minute looking at his partially filled pillowcase and stack of magazines. What just happened to him flashed through his mind? They really did want him here and he could stay, at least for a while. Today was not the day he had to leave so he had more time to make a better plan. Right now he was feeling better. He was feeling wanted and secure knowing that he was loved.

As he looked over to his dresser he saw the folded paper with the bible verses he had gotten from Sunday School. As he stood there he thought for a minute about the prayer he had in the grove behind the barn. He prayed to Jesus and asked for help. Could this really be an answer to his prayer? It hit him, as he stood there, that's how prayer works. You ask and God takes over, just like that. Now he got it. He would always pray when he needed help. Now he knew for sure that Jesus was listening to him.

With all of that going through his mind he started to unpack and put his things back where they came from. Now he just wanted to get back outside and play with Terry whom he thought he was going leave behind. He could still play with his best friend, something he enjoyed doing more than anything else at all.

After Billy was unpacked he emerged from his room. He stopped as he saw Ruth unpacking the mattress. It took her a while as she was trying to preserve the wrapping paper in order to use it again to repack the mattress when the baby left. She and Samuel learned a long time ago to not be wasteful, as they didn't have a lot of money to replace things.

Instead of going downstairs and outside Billy took a little detour. He walked over to where Ruth was struggling to pull the mattress out of the wrapping that was only open at one end. Taking hold of the wrapping paper Billy held as Ruth pulled out the mattress.

"Thank you, Billy," Ruth said. "You go outside now and play. I'll call you when lunch is ready."

"Okay," Billy said and bounced down the stairs on his way outside. Ruth smiled knowing she had forged a new relationship with this little guy that she now hoped could stay with them for a long time.

CHAPTER 16

Lunch was over and everyone was extremely quiet. They were now each doing something different to pass the time until Mrs. Adams arrived. Ruth was folding some baby clothes that she found and had washed and hung on the clothesline. Samuel was sitting in the living room reading the Sunday paper that he never finished Sunday. Normally he would be finishing in the field and then come home to get the eggs ready for the egg route the next day. Today was special and he took a short break from it all.

Billy, Martha and Rachel were playing tinker toys on the living room floor. Martha and Billy were tolerating Rachel's participation, as she couldn't pickup up a stick without disturbing the whole pile. The whole game strategy was to pick up a stick while not moving any others. They knew it was just for fun and they wouldn't keep score this time.

It was a beautiful spring day yet no one wanted to leave the house until Mrs. Adams came. It was nearing the time she would be there. Ruth was now sitting at the kitchen table. Her eyes were glued to the clock on the wall. With each passing minute the tension grew. It was now 2:55 p.m. In five minutes she could be driving in their driveway. Ruth remembered the last time Mrs. Adams came and she was twenty minutes late. Hopefully, this time that wouldn't happen as an additional twenty minutes would be painful.

Just then Terry started barking outside. The children all jumped to their feet and were in the kitchen in a flash. Samuel was right behind them. Ruth and Samuel had eye contact with a little bit of fear on each of their faces. They all moved to the porch to go outside and greet Mrs. Adams.

Sure enough, it was Mrs. Adams' car coming down the drive. Billy grabbed a piece of Terry's hair on the back of his neck to hold him back from running out to the car and being a nuisance. His overfriendliness often got him in trouble with Samuel and Billy wanted to avoid that from happening. It usually got Terry locked up in the shed until the coast was clear of any visitors.

Mrs. Adams stopped the car in exactly the same place she did when bringing Billy. She got out of the car and opened the back door where she removed a small basket covered with baby blankets. Ruth and Samuel walked closer to the car.

Mrs. Adams said, "Let's take the baby inside before we open the blankets. The air might be a little chilly for the baby out here."

"Okay", was the unison response from Samuel and Ruth.

The adults headed toward the porch steps and then into the house with the children following behind. When they got into the kitchen Mrs. Adams put the basket on the kitchen table. Samuel stood Rachel up on a chair so she could see.

Mrs. Adams opened the blankets and revealed the smallest baby Ruth and Samuel had ever seen. It started to move and gave a huge yawn. Mrs. Adams told them that the baby was very fragile but the doctors had released it saying it was good to go.

She then added, "Handle him carefully but, don't be afraid. He is the same as any other baby. All bodily functions are normal. He just needs to grow a little and with some tender loving care he will be alright."

Ruth was nodding during Mrs. Adams' dissertation never taking her eyes off the baby. Mrs. Adams asked if she wanted to pick him up. Ruth immediately reached into the basket carefully picking up the baby with both hands. When she picked the baby up she leaned him against her bosom and looked at Mrs. Adams with a huge smile.

"What is his name?" Ruth asked.

Mrs. Adams looked back with a nervous grin and said, "He doesn't have a name. The mother didn't want to name him since he was being adopted. His birth certificate says Baby Smith, as Smith was her last name. The adoptive parents will be giving him a name. I'm just not certain what that is. So, in the meantime, Baby Smith will have to do."

Ruth and Samuel were stunned, as never did they know of a baby that didn't have a name. It would only be a week so they'd have to get by without the name.

Samuel asked if the adoptive parents were Christian. That was very important to Samuel and Ruth knowing that as a child of God in a Christian home this baby would be raised to know Jesus as his Savior. Mrs. Adams assured them that the adoptive parents were Christian and she was certain they would raise this baby in a Christian manner. That brought a sense of relief to both Samuel and Ruth. Knowing this would make it easier to give this baby up to the new parents when they got back into town. They were both looking at each other with smiles of contentment on their faces.

Mrs. Adams then turned and looked at Billy.

"Billy, could you and I take a walk? I'd like to speak with you for a little bit."

Billy said, "Okay" and started toward the door.

He felt at ease based on what Ruth told him that morning when she said Mrs. Adams would want to speak with him. They both headed out the door together.

When they got outside Mrs. Adams said, "Let's sit over here in the lawn chairs."

They both settled into the lawn chairs and Mrs. Adams asked, "Billy, are things alright with you? Are the Schultzes nice to you?"

Billy replied, "Yes, I'm okay. The Schultzes are nice people."

"That's good", Mrs. Adams said. "Do you like it here?"

"Yes," was Billy's simple response.

"Do you need anything, Billy?", she continued.

"No, I'm okay, I don't need anything. Mrs. Schultz bought me a pair of new trousers and a new shirt for church on Sunday."

Mrs. Adams knew at that moment that she had a new set of foster parents that were a perfect fit for the system. Generally people didn't purchase new clothes for their foster children until they got their first check from the Welfare system. This was a good sign and her instincts about the Schultzes were right on target.

"Well, Billy if you are okay and things are going well for you, I'll see you on my next visit. If you do need anything have Mrs. Schultz call me?"

She then got up and walked back into the house. After saying a few goodbyes to the Schultz family she was on her way. They were now left with the new baby to handle things themselves.

Ruth was holding him as they all waved as Mrs. Adams drove out. Rachel was hanging onto Ruth's apron. This was a little unsettling for the baby of the family. With this happening so quickly there hadn't been time to explain the baby to Rachel and Martha. There was bound to be some confusion, especially with little Rachel. Here they were a family of six almost overnight, something that Ruth and Samuel put from their minds long ago and now they were living it, even though it was temporary.

Ruth, Samuel and the girls went back into the house. Ruth sat down on a kitchen chair still holding Baby Smith. Rachel and Martha had lots of questions as they all watched the baby sleep. This would be a new experience for all of them. Ruth explained how they would have to be very careful with the baby, as it was frail. They certainly didn't want anything to happen to it. She also explained how this was not one of their dolls and they could not pick it up or play with it. They could watch it but not touch it unless she was there with them.

At that moment Martha, who was now also standing next to Ruth, reached her finger over very slowly and touched the baby's hand. Ruth watched her every move very intently. As Martha's finger touched the little hand the baby opened his hand and grabbed her finger. She was startled but didn't pull back.

She just giggled and said, "Look Mommy, he wants to hold my finger."

Ruth smiled and said nothing. Rachel then made the same move but a little more aggressively. This time Ruth stopped her hand from touching the baby, which put a scowl on Rachel's face. Ruth knew that upset her and decided to help. She took Rachel's hand and slowly and carefully ran it up the small arm of the baby whose soft skin made Rachel giggle.

Out of concern for the baby Ruth said, "Okay, let's give the baby a rest now. You go out and play."

Everyone then got the message and left to go outside, except Samuel who was content to watch Ruth hold the baby with such a loving look of contentment on her face. Ruth's joy in holding the baby was certainly visible. It was like something that had been missing in her life that was now fulfilled. She didn't even realize what she was missing until she held Baby Smith. Her last opportunity to hold a baby was when Rachel was an infant. But, then she had another miscarriage and Rachel had grown out of the baby phase.

She knew she wouldn't have another baby and that made it even harder to accept. She knew God was a merciful God and he was molding her life. But, not being able to hold the children she lost and not the possibility of another baby to replace them left her with an unexplainable empty feeling. She didn't want to spoil this new baby but she felt like holding him all the time.

Ruth looked at Samuel and said, "We can't keep calling this child Baby Smith. He has to have a name even if it's just one we use."

"I don't know," Samuel said, "It isn't our place to give the child a name."

"I'm not talking about a permanent name," Ruth said defending her idea, "We don't even have to tell anyone, it's just for us. I like the name David, don't you?"

Samuel was giving her a funny look wondering where she was going with this. Why was a name so important?

Ruth continued, "David fought the giant Goliath and beat him. I think our young David will need to be a giant killer as this little guy takes on the big old world with nothing more than his willpower. He came into this world early to get a head start and he needs a fitting name."

"Ruth, if you want to give this little guy a name that only we use, go right ahead. It can be a Nickname. When he is gone it won't matter what we called him. Just be careful you don't get too attached as he won't be staying that long," Samuel said with great concern.

He knew how hard their last loss had been for Ruth and that was his main concern in taking in foster children. It was his ultimate hope that these children would fill a need she had rather than be another chance to open old wounds.

"I know Samuel," Ruth responded with a hint of disappointment as she was already getting attached.

Samuel may have guessed but he never really knew how much losing their babies affected Ruth as she always displayed such self-control trying to not let her disappointment show. The week would be a true test of her resilience.

CHAPTER 17

*B*aby David was in the baby basket taking a nap. He slept a lot, which was good, as he needed lots of rest in order to keep growing. Grandpa and Grandma Schultz came over to see the baby. In fact, Grandma agreed to take the baby upstairs to Samuel and Ruth's room and put him in the crib for a nap. She said she would stay there with him. They had a nice rocking chair in their room that faced the window where you could see for miles. She just loved the view.

Grandpa had gone home and brought back some knitting for Anna to work on while she watched the baby. By doing this it allowed Samuel and Ruth to get the eggs ready to take on the egg route in the morning. Ruth and Samuel worked on the candling process to be sure they sorted the eggs and took only the best along on the route.

Ruth brought something up that perhaps they were both thinking, "Samuel, I'm not sure I can go on the egg route tomorrow. I may have to stay home and take care of the baby."

Samuel nodded in agreement and said, "I was thinking about that. It might be best to not take the baby out much with him being so small. I also don't think Mom should be watching him in case something happens she may not know what to do. And, I am always concerned that something could happen to her and then what would happen to the baby? I can go alone. It will take longer but I think I can do it."

Ruth had an idea, "What if Billy went along?"

"I never thought of that," Samuel agreed, "He just might be able to help. Do you think he would want to go along?"

Ruth nodded and said, "I just think he would like that. Why don't you ask him"?

Agreeing with her, Samuel got up and went outside to find Billy. He was busy throwing a stick for Terry to catch in the front yard.

"Billy, can you come here please?" Samuel called to him. As Billy came close Samuel asked the question, "Would you like to come with me on the egg route tomorrow and help me?"

Without taking a breath Billy said, "Oh yes, I would like that. What do I have to do?"

"You can help me carry some of the eggs and collect the money," was Samuel's response. "Okay," was all Billy had to say and they each went back to what they had been doing.

When Samuel got back to the house Ruth was on the phone dialing her brother Albert. She remembered that she told him he didn't need to go to town to take her mother grocery shopping as she would stop when they went to town for the egg route. Now that wouldn't be possible so they needed to make other plans.

"Hello, Albert?" she had reached him. "Albert I need to talk with you about my promise to take Mom grocery shopping tomorrow. A little something has come up."

There was a pause and Samuel knew Albert was asking what that 'little' something was.

"Well, we got another call from the Welfare Department and they had a crisis and needed our help. A baby was born over the weekend that was scheduled to be adopted and the adoptive parents are out of town for a few days. They asked us to keep the baby and I can't leave it at home with Grandma Schultz. She's been sick and it's so small, we shouldn't be taking it out. What do you think we can do about Mom and grocery shopping this week?"

Ruth and her brother Albert had a great relationship. She respected him. He was always good to her. She was now listening to his response and after a short time replied.

"Oh, that would be great Albert. I am so sorry about the change in plans; I know I promised I would take Mom this week. You are the best for helping me out."

Now there was another pause and then she responded, "Yes, I know. This is only going to be for a week or less and the adoptive parents will be back in town to take the baby. I know we have so much work around here and with the addition of Billy I will be careful to not take on too much."

Albert was concerned for her, as he knew how much she had been through in the few years she and Samuel have been married. That's what big brothers do; they protect their little sisters.

"Yes, Albert, Billy is doing fine. He is going to help Samuel on the egg route tomorrow. He is always more than willing to help us when we ask. He has a lot on his mind and seems to be very sensitive, even though he tries to keep it all inside. He still is just a ten year old boy and that does show sometimes."

There was another pause and then she held the phone out toward Samuel, who was back to working on candling the eggs.

"Samuel, Albert wants to talk with you. Samuel put down the eggs in his hand and walked over to the phone.

"Hello, what can I do for you Albert?" was his opening.

Then there was a long pause. Ruth was standing near watching Samuel and his facial expression; it went from being emotionless to having a puzzling look to a very large smile.

Then he spoke, "Of course, I will take it. Yes, that's about how much I would need for the ten acres. I wasn't certain we would be able to afford to buy it this year and with the season now being a little late to plant I wasn't certain I wanted to take the risk. This is so great. I'll stop over on my way back from town tomorrow, if that will work for you. I'll take the pickup truck on the route, I don't think it's going to rain and we'll pick it up. Thank you so very much."

There was another short pause and Samuel said, "OK, I'll tell her, good bye."

After he hung up the phone, Samuel stood there a little while holding on to the receiver on the wall before he took his hand off. Ruth was wondering what Albert told him that put him in this state.

So, she asked, "What did Albert want?"

Samuel looked at her with a huge grin and said, "It seems that as he was moving some of the seed corn sacks around he found that there had been some water damage from a leak in his roof that he wasn't aware of. It got some of the sacks wet and when he called the seed company they told him he couldn't sell and should dump it. He said he didn't think the damage was too great and maybe about a fourth of each sack might have to be thrown away but, if I wanted to sort through it he would give me all of the sacks he couldn't sell."

Looking right at Ruth he said, "This is a miracle. We can now plant the field and don't have to risk losing the money I was concerned about spending to buy the seed. What a blessing."

Ruth came close to Samuel and did something they rarely did in public. She gave him a huge hug. When she had her arms around him he reciprocated by putting his arms around her and actually picked her up and swung her around. They both laughed as he put her down. Ruth was so proud of Samuel. To a certain extent he reminded her of her father who even though he had struggles in getting his farm started and building its value, he always had a positive attitude never getting down at the slightest disappointment. Plus, both her father and Samuel had a strong faith in the Lord, who always took care of them in some way or another.

They now both walked back over to the area where they had been working on candling the eggs. As they did that Ruth remembered she hadn't told Samuel about her conversation with Albert.

"It turns out that Albert and Sarah had planned to go to the city on Wednesday anyway so, if Mom can wait one more day, which she'll have to, they will take her shopping. She won't like the idea that she missed meeting Billy, but she'll have plenty of time to meet him. At least I think she will. I'm just not sure how long he'll be with us. Keeping welfare children seems to be full of surprises. It doesn't seem like it's only been a week since Billy came to us."

Samuel was nodding in agreement as he kept working with the eggs making certain they were packed carefully in their cartons.

Ruth continued, "Albert is going to call Mom and make the new arrangements. I'm sort of happy he was willing to make the call. I somehow think she wouldn't like the idea of me taking in little David and I don't need to get a lecture right now. I know she cares but, I'm okay just putting in this week and we can talk about it when I go to town next time."

The eggs were now all in cartons and packed into larger containers.

Samuel said, "I am going to lay down some quilts on the truck bed to give it a little more cushion. I'll have to take the truck so I can pick up the seed on the way home. I want to be certain the eggs have the entire cushion they need for the ride. We'll be driving very slowly into town. As I remember on the ride to Albert's there are a few nice pot holes on the road."

Samuel then left to go outside. Ruth headed up the steps to check on Baby David and Grandma Schultz. When Ruth got to the bedroom door she could hear snoring. As she looked in she saw Grandma Schultz with her head back on the rocker sleeping soundly. She walked over to the crib and there was the baby looking up at her with a big smile on his face. He giggled a little and moved all over. What a happy baby he was. All she could think about was how lucky the new adoptive parents are to get such a happy baby as this. He might be small but he has a huge heart she thought as she picked him up and held him up resting against her shoulder.

Ruth looked over at Grandma Schultz and she was reassured that she couldn't leave Baby David alone with her as she would not be alert enough if something happened. It's different when she watches the other children, as there is always Grandpa Schultz who could help if they needed it. Caring for an infant is much different and at least for this week it would be her own responsibility. And, she loved the thought of it.

CHAPTER 18

The next morning Samuel got up extra early. He milked the cows and instead of coming in for breakfast he took out the pickup truck and drove to Greenville. There he met Ben Bartlett at the back door of his grocery store. He needed to get some dry ice to take with him on his egg route to keep the chickens fresh he would be delivering. Ben always had some extra for the farmers who would stop by for the same need as Samuel had that day.

He filled the wooden cases he brought with him, that were lined with a canvas. He then covered the dry ice with the canvas and covered the entire case with several quilts. The dry ice would keep the chickens cool for hours as he traveled his route to deliver them.

He thanked Ben Bartlett and told him to put it on his bill. He promised to stop back later in the week, when Ruth picked up groceries, and pay his bill. That's how things worked. The grocer kept a tab for each of the farmers who would pay when they had new cash flow from selling something they grew or raised on their farms. The trust level was high and everyone involved in this business relationship was honorable and trustworthy. He got what he needed and headed back home for the busy day ahead of him.

When he got back home he parked the truck right by the back door and headed inside. Ruth had the children up, dressed and eating breakfast. Billy was eating fast as he didn't want to be late for the egg route or worse yet, be left behind. Samuel sat in his chair at the head of the table. Ruth had filled Samuel's plate with a couple of fried eggs, a few strips of bacon and a couple slices of toast. She even took the time to butter it and spread some of her homemade strawberry jelly on it. Samuel loved her strawberry jelly and was happy there was still some left from last year's batch. By the end of summer they might run out but for now he was just thankful there was still some left for his eating enjoyment.

Soon Samuel looked like a much bigger Billy as he was downing his food at a record pace. He sipped a little coffee between bites. While chewing he looked up and saw Billy doing the very same thing. He smiled, put down his cup and started to laugh. Everyone looked up wondering what he was laughing about.

He finally said, "I guess Billy and me are in a food chewing race to see who can chew the least before swallowing. I thought I was in the lead but I think Billy has officially passed me."

Billy was slow to look up as he was still engaged in his fast pace eating. He finally realized what Samuel said and he started to giggle along with everyone else. He really was so focused on his eating that he sort of lost touch with how fast he was going. He was so excited about going along on the egg route that he could hardly hold himself down in his chair.

Everyone finally stopped laughing and slowly went back to finishing breakfast.

Rachel was still giggling as she looked at Samuel and said, "You and Billy are eating fast. You are both so silly," and then she giggled a little more.

Ruth pointed to the food in front of Rachel, then to her mouth, as a silent instruction for her to get back to eating. It was a nice moment for everyone. It was feeling more and more like a family and now Billy was officially included. They laughed together at themselves and there's nothing that bonds a family more than that. What a nice way to start the day.

When breakfast was over Samuel looked at Billy and said, "Okay son, it's time to go."

Calling a little boy son was nothing uncommon for Samuel he used that expression a lot. However, it did catch Billy by surprise. Never had he heard Samuel say that to him before. What did it mean? It took him back. He was stuck in his tracks.

Finally he heard Samuel say, "Billy, we need to go now. Grab the lunch Mom made and let's go."

Now Samuel called Ruth Mom. What did that mean? Why did he say these things today? He was so confused. Were the Schultzes going to adopt him? Did they really want him or were they just being nice to him? He still has a Dad, how could anyone want him or adopt him? Tons of things were just racing through his mind. He now tried to collect himself and started off toward the door. He'd have to think about this some more. Right now he'd better get going as Mr. Schultz needed him today and he didn't want to get left behind.

Samuel and Billy had all of the eggs loaded in the back of the pickup and the chickens were safely packed inside the homemade icebox Samuel created. Now they needed to get going as time was ticking into the morning and they needed to get the eggs delivered before the heat of day arrived.

They were now on the road and Samuel was driving extremely carefully watching for those pesky potholes that could break the eggs in the back of the truck. Billy was all of a sudden very talkative and inquisitive.

"Mr. Schultz?" Billy asked, "Why do we deliver eggs and chickens to peoples homes? Can't they just go to the grocery store for those things?"

Billy sure had a way of making Samuel smile with his naïve knowledge of country living.

Samuel answered saying, "Oh, yes they could go to the store and buy them. But, they want fresh country eggs and chickens. Plus they know where they came from if they buy them from us. I also think they feel they are getting a better price and helping us country folk make a living."

"Oh," was Billy's answer, as he went back to looking out the window pondering what Samuel said after breakfast when he called him son.

As they got into the city the houses were getting closer together, the streets were getting populated with cars and there were people all over walking down the sidewalks. This was certainly a better part of town than where Billy lived with his father. Things looked clean and well kept. You couldn't see garbage cans in the front yard. The houses were painted and there weren't broken down fences between houses. If there was a fence there weren't any broken boards and they were nicely painted. The grass was cut and they didn't have big chunks out of their front steps or sidewalks. This was so different than what Billy was used to seeing.

Samuel took a turn off the main street and came to a stop just outside of a house in the middle of the block.

"Here we are, Billy," were his words. "This is where we start. Let's get out and I'll grab a case of eggs. You bring the money pouch. When we get to the door we will take out the number of cartons we usually leave with each person. Since Ruth isn't with us I may not totally know which of the customers ordered chickens. I forgot the list that Ruth made for us so we'll have to use the honor system and ask them. When they give us the money you put it in the pouch and tie it shut so you won't accidentally drop any as we go to the next place. Do you think you can do that?"

"I think I can," was Billy's response, which had just a little tone of doubt in his voice.

He was actually very nervous about doing this. He wanted to but more importantly he didn't want to make a mistake and make Mr. Schultz think he wasn't a good helper. He kept telling himself, *'just do as he says and you'll be alright.'*

Now they were walking down the first sidewalk up to the front door. Before Billy was able to knock, the door opened.

A lady stepped out and said, "Samuel, I was hoping you'd make it today." She started looking around and finally said, "Is Ruth with you?"

"Not today, Mrs. Gregory," Samuel explained, "she had to stay at home and watch a newborn we have in our charge for about a week."

Mrs. Gregory then looked down at Billy and said, "And, who is this nice looking young man you have with you today?"

"This is Billy, he is also staying with us for a while," Samuel explained.

Mrs. Gregory continued, "So, why do you have these children to care for? You said a week right?"

She then looked back down at Billy and asked him, "And where do you live and is that where you are going back to in a week?"

Billy found a lump developing in his throat. He so hoped he didn't start to cry. Why did she ask that question? It was the baby that was leaving in a week. Or, was he also leaving and he just didn't know it. He hated what was happening to him. He was so happy to help with the egg route and now he was feeling terrible again.

Samuel spoke, "Oh no, Mrs. Gregory. Billy will be with us longer. It's just the baby that is leaving. Ruth and I decided to become foster parents and Billy is our first foster child."

"Oh, how nice of you to do that. Billy I hope you are enjoying your stay with the Schultzes," was her final comment about personal matters.

All Billy could focus on was her new comment about his living with the Schultzes being just a 'stay', making it sound like it was a short visit. Maybe that's exactly what it really was intended to be. He better go back to getting his plans in order about leaving on his own.

After that bit of conversation Samuel told Billy to take two cartons of eggs out for Mrs. Gregory. He would go to the truck and get the two chickens Mrs. Gregory said she ordered from Ruth on their last visit. He told Mrs. Gregory what the cost would be. She went in the house to get the money while Samuel put down the case of eggs on the porch steps to go get the chickens. Billy took two cartons of eggs out of the case and put them on the chair next to where they were standing.

Mrs. Gregory came back to the porch and handed Billy the money, which he carefully put in the money pouch tying it shut. By now Samuel was on his way back with the two chickens he had wrapped so carefully the day before. He handed her the chickens. Billy pointed to the two cartons of eggs he had put on the chair.

Samuel asked Billy if he had looked at the eggs to make sure none were broken. Billy looked embarrassed, as he didn't know he was supposed to do that. He reluctantly shook his head no. Samuel picked up each carton one by one and opened them inspecting to make sure none were broken.

"These look okay, Mrs. Gregory", was his comment as he put them back down and stepped back to pick up the remaining case of eggs.

He started down the walkway with Billy following right behind as Mrs. Gregory waved good-bye. It was quite apparent to Billy now that Samuel was in a very serious frame of mind. He had a job to do and his mind was solely on that. Billy knew he needed to stay up with him and do all of the little extra's Samuel brought him along to do. And, they needed to keep moving as they were on a schedule.

The morning went by quickly. They only had to replace one carton of eggs that got broken on the trip. That meant that Samuel had brought along more than he needed and would have to take them home again. He also had one chicken left when they were all done.

A couple of people weren't home and usually they would leave a note to leave the delivery at neighbors but there wasn't any note this time. That wasn't totally unusual. Maybe they had enough eggs from the last delivery and they forgot they ordered a chicken. Or maybe Ruth just butchered one more than they needed. Whatever the reason there was now one left and the ice was starting to melt.

Samuel had an idea so nothing would go to waste. They were only a few blocks from Ruth's mother's house. She would take some of the left over eggs and she could probably use the chicken as well. They could stop there on their way out of town. When you live on the farm you don't waste anything, if you can avoid it. So, Samuel thought this was a good move.

He quickly told Billy what he was going to do. He knew it would be a surprise for his mother-in-law but, he didn't want to take the chance of the chicken spoiling as well as there were more eggs left over than they could use. Billy was a little apprehensive about the visit but the day had been full of surprises so why not one more.

After driving a couple of blocks Samuel turned and soon they were driving into the driveway of Mrs. Becker, Ruth's mother. There she was, sitting on the screened in porch in her rocking chair reading the paper. She was immediately up from her chair and holding the door open calling out to Samuel.

"Samuel, what a nice surprise, I didn't expect you today. I just got off the phone with Ruth to see how things were going. Albert called yesterday telling me about the change in plans because of the baby. What are you doing here?"

Samuel was uncovering the back of the truck to get the leftover eggs out that he handed to Billy, who was standing by his side, not wanting to go to the house without him. Then, he opened up the box with the ice and removed the chicken.

Samuel called over to Mrs. Becker, "I had one too many chickens and a few extra eggs I thought you could use. I didn't want to chicken to spoil on the way home as most of my ice is starting to melt."

"That is very nice of you Samuel. Come in, I'll make you a cup of coffee."

By now they were walking toward the house and her eyes were glued on Billy.

"This must be William," she said. No one ever called him William and he looked up immediately at her.

She continued, "My father's name was William and I think it's a special name reserved for special people."

Billy was astonished at the comparison. She actually compared him to a family member. What was so special about his name? He had never given it any thought before this. He was very pleased with her compliment and his precious, ten year old smile, came to life.

Samuel handed her the chicken and said, "We don't have time for any coffee, I have to stop at Albert's on the way home and pick up some seed he is holding for me. I want to get home with the left over eggs. I had hoped to sell them but some of our customers weren't home today. I only have six dozen left. Do you know of anyone who might use them so I could get them out of the truck where I want to put the seed bags? I'm afraid they will get broken. Here are a couple of dozen for you. That only leaves four dozen more."

Billy reached up with the two cartons of eggs. She had her hands full with the chicken so she said, "Come in Billy and we'll put them in the refrigerator. Samuel, I'm not sure about the other four dozen. Let me call Mrs. Christianson next door and ask her. I'll do that when we go inside."

They now walked through the hallway from the front door to the kitchen passing the living room on the way. It was a small kitchen with a big pantry where she kept her refrigerator There she put the eggs. She then opened up the freezer and put the chicken there. Walking to the phone she called Mrs. Christianson, her next-door neighbor, whose family went to the same church as Mrs. Becker. They were a young family but took a liking to Mrs. Becker and helped her out a lot around her place, especially since her husband died last year.

When she got off the phone she had a big smile on her face as she said, "Mrs. Christianson will take all four dozen. In fact, she would really like six dozen so I'll give up the two dozen you just gave to me. I can wait until next week to do some of the baking I was planning on doing and I have a few eggs left for breakfast. Mrs. Christianson would like some herself and she is on her way up to church and said she would like to give some to our pastor and his family. That's a nice idea. Samuel, would you mind taking them next door. You can collect from her when you get there."

Samuel nodded his head and she took the two dozen she had just put in the refrigerator and handed them to him.

Samuel was heading toward the front door when Mrs. Becker said one more thing. "Do you think I could come back with you for a few days and help Ruth around the house since she has the baby to take care of? I know that your mother isn't well and I'm sure Ruth could use the help. I was going to ask Albert, when he comes to town tomorrow if he would take me out to your place. This would save him that trip. Plus he wouldn't have to make a special trip for my groceries tomorrow either."

Samuel thought for a second and said, "If you don't mind riding in my old truck with me and Billy? It will be a bumpy ride and we will need to stop at Albert's place before we go home. I'm sure Ruth would love to see you and certainly could use the help."

"I don't mind the ride" she replied, "I'll get packed while you go next door. Billy why don't you go with Samuel while I go upstairs or you can wait on the porch."

Billy followed Samuel right out the door. They went next door and conducted their business. When they got back Mrs. Becker was at the door with her hat and coat and suitcase in hand. Samuel took the suitcase and waited while she locked the door. He put the suitcase in the back of the pickup and soon they were off. Samuel was thinking Ruth would be both happy to see her mother and a little irritated that she didn't have advance notice of her arrival. Since he knew the good outweighed the bad he would live with Ruth's temporary look of disapproval. He thought this was a wonderful turn of events that would benefit everyone, including Ruth's mother, who probably gets lonesome living alone and would love to see her youngest daughter.

The trip to Albert and Sarah's was filled with questions from Ruth's mother to Samuel about the baby. She hadn't asked Ruth, as she didn't want to spend that much time on the phone, as it was long distance. Samuel answered her questions the best he could. Some of her questions were the same ones he had himself but hadn't asked so he couldn't provide answers. They'd both have to wait for the answers when they got home.

CHAPTER 19

*R*uth spent the day doing nothing but watching Baby David. Most of the time she held him close, just wanting to feel his presence. She knew that wasn't a good idea, as the baby couldn't always be held when he got to his new home. She just couldn't help herself. There was something about having this newborn in her arms that was fulfilling something missing in her life. Yes, she had experience with newborns when Martha and Rachel were born but this was different somehow. She couldn't explain it but it was just different.

Knowing that the baby was being given away left a sort of sadness inside of her. She kept wondering how anyone could give something so precious and so defenseless away. She and Samuel had lost their precious babies and would have given the world to have just five minutes of being able to hold them. Baby David was at least being given a second chance with adoptive parents. He would live a life with people who really wanted him.

Ruth started to think back on the episode with Billy who thought he was being taken away again. How unsettling, she thought, for such a young child to be tossed about from home to home not knowing what to expect next. His young heart was so broken that he couldn't hold back his emotions. How would he grow up? Would he ever trust anyone again? Would he ever be able to settle down and not be on edge wondering what would happen to him next? Maybe he too would be given adoptive parents who would love him and bring peace to his life.

He'd only been with them for a very short time and he was already starting to blend into their family. They will certainly miss him when he leaves. Maybe he would be able to stay with them for a while. She thought that everyone, Samuel, Martha, Rachel and even Samuel's parents were getting attached to him and would feel a loss if he left. They'd have to get used to that because that's what it's like caring for foster children. If Billy left she was sure Mrs. Adams would bring out another child for them to help raise.

Then she started to wonder how she would feel when Baby David left. She knew that she had already, in just a day, made a bond with this new life. He was in such a need to make a connection with a mother and his real mother wasn't there. She wondered what his birth mother was like. Was she so young that she couldn't care for a baby? Was this child just born out of wedlock and the mother didn't want to face the embarrassment of bringing up a child as a single parent? Did she already have more children then she could handle and just gave the next one up? Ruth would never know. She wondered if Baby David would ever meet her, as he too would wonder who she was. Maybe his new parents will never tell him. She just knew that his mother would miss having the joy of seeing him grow up and felt sad for her.

She had to stop herself before she became obsessed. He was leaving in a few days and she would let him go to people who wanted him. He'd be just fine and wouldn't need her any longer. Is this how caring for foster children will be? She would feel pain when he left, she wouldn't be able to help herself. She would feel some pain if Billy left as well. Would she be able to endure it again and again if they kept caring for foster children? It seems like this is a role that was meant for them. God would help them through it, just like He helped them when they lost their own babies.

What she and Samuel did know is that their lives were in God's hands. He picked them up when they thought the low points in their lives had taken them so low they couldn't pick themselves up. They needed their merciful heavenly Father and He had been there for them. Ruth was convinced that their new venture with foster children was all in God's plan and she trusted that it was right for them.

Maybe she would put Baby David down for a bit in his crib. No, she just couldn't take him upstairs and leave him there alone. What she would do is put him in the basket that Mrs. Adams brought him in yesterday. She got it from the living room and put Baby David down in it. He fussed a little but then settled down in a sound sleep. He had been up and alert for the past hour or so and it was time for a restful sleep. Ruth put him on the kitchen table, where she could see him at anytime. She then walked over to the refrigerator and took out some hamburger. She wasn't quite certain when Samuel and Billy would be home but they would probably be there for supper and she would have it ready for them.

Ruth looked at the clock and it was already three o'clock. She knew the two girls would be taking a nap about now. Grandma Schultz must have put them down in her own bed rather than bring them home. The girls loved their grandparents. She just wished her mother would be closer so they could see her more. They did get to go along on the egg route and would stay with their Grandma Becker for the few hours when she and Samuel would handle their route. That gave them some quality time with her mother.

Ruth was so happy that both Samuel's parents and her mother simply loved having her children with them. If they could have them visit more often they certainly would be happy. It seemed that even though Samuel's parents see the children practically every day they never got tired of their visits. For that Ruth was so thankful because it gave her the ability to do many more things to help Samuel around the farm knowing her children will being well cared for at all times.

※

Next door Martha and Rachel were up from their nap and were re-energized. They loved spending the afternoon with their Grandpa and Grandma Schultz. Grandpa was now playing cards with them, one of their favorite events. They were pretty good at playing Crazy Eights and Go Fish. When they got bored they would insist on playing Slap Jack, a wild and crazy game. It would usually end up with both of them laughing so hard that they would literally roll on the floor.

It took good reflexes to slap the Jacks before your opponent. The only good thing about having slower reflexes is that when your opponent slapped the Jack first your hand generally ended on top of theirs and you could slap it as hard as you wanted. Martha and Rachel would laugh and laugh as they tried and tried but, generally couldn't beat the adults playing along, especially Grandpa Schultz. Sometimes Grandpa would let them get the first hit and then he would carefully put his hand on top of theirs not letting go until they burst into laughter.

When the girls had been napping earlier Grandpa Schultz went over to the farm and did some of Ruth's outside chores. That way she could stay in and do her inside chores while watching Baby David. He finished his work and was enjoying every minute he had with his granddaughters after their nap. They were full of life and he loved how they giggled and showed how much they loved him and Anna. They brought life to their house when they were there and things were always interesting. He just loved having them around.

CHAPTER 20

Ruth finished making supper. She made a hot dish and it was now in the oven. The aroma had already permeated the entire house. Anyone within 50 feet of the house could smell this great scent. Her family loved her hot dishes so she made them at least once a week. It also was easy to serve if they were eating in shifts, as it would stay hot in the over for a long time. Tonight they may not be eating at the same time so it seemed like the perfect meal. She already fed Baby David and he was content enough to take yet another nap. He was sleeping soundly when she heard Samuel's truck coming down the driveway. She walked over to the kitchen window to take a look to confirm it was Samuel.

As she watched the truck getting closer she could see there were two adults in the cab. She was a little confused and wondered who it might be. As they got closer it became clear it was an older lady with a hat. Then, all of a sudden, she realized it was her mother. She recognized her white hair combed back into a pug with one of her many hats she always wore when going out. She was a gracious and stylish lady who always carried herself with dignity.

Ruth loved her mother and was so happy she was here, no matter what the reason, although her curiosity was peaked as to why she came. It wasn't that long ago that she talked with her on the phone and she didn't say a word about coming to visit, especially with Samuel who wasn't even going to stop at her house this week.

Ruth picked up Baby David and started to walk outside to greet her mother. Samuel stopped by the back porch door and her mother and Billy got out the passengers door. Her mother was walking toward Ruth with a huge smile on her face.

Ruth said, "Mom, what are you doing here?"

Her mother responded with reaching for her daughter to give her a hug. She grabbed her around the neck and gave her a kiss on her cheek.

Mrs. Becker then stepped back looking at Baby David saying, "Well now, you have added two more children since I saw you a couple of weeks ago. I'd say you have accomplished quite a bit in such a short time. I just had to come see for myself. I already met that charming Billy. Who is this very young fellow?"

"This is David", Ruth replied. "That isn't his real name. I gave it to him. He doesn't have a name yet and I just needed to call him something. I felt David was appropriate since he has the giant world to face, like Goliath."

Ruth just kept talking trying to explain her act of naming and seemed to be apologizing at the same time.

"I know it might not be right for me to name him when he will be getting new parents soon. When he leaves here, that name will stay with us."

Ruth looked at her mother with a pleading look on her face.

Her mother put her hand on Ruth's shoulder and said, "I think it's okay Ruth. You just need to be careful you don't get too attached and make it hard for yourself when he has to leave."

"I know mother," Ruth replied while looking down at Baby David with great compassion.

Samuel walked around the truck and picked up Mrs. Becker's suitcase and brought it to the porch steps where he set it down. Billy was standing next to the truck watching the interaction between Ruth and her mother. He could see the genuine love between the two. He was very attentive to how people interacted and had been amazed, since he got to the Schultz farm, as to how lovingly they related to each other. They didn't say it in words but they certainly showed it in their actions.

Ruth looked at Billy and gave him an instruction, "Billy, please run over to Grandpa and Grandma Schultz and tell Martha and Rachel they should come home now as we will be having supper soon. You can tell Grandpa and Grandma they can join us, if they would like."

"Okay", Billy said as he started running through the shrubs toward the little house next door.

As he ran out of sight Mrs. Becker looked at Ruth and said, "that is such a fine little boy. It is so sad to think that he has been put into the welfare system. I hope he finds a good home with people who will love him and he can then avoid any more disappointments in his life. He seems to be coping with it all very well. I'm sure it's been good for him to be with you, Samuel and your girls."

"He is a very interesting boy," Ruth responded. "He has so much emotion built up inside but he rarely shows it on the outside. I think he is much more sensitive that anyone knows. I too wish nothing but the best for him. In the meantime, we are enjoying his curiosity and desire to learn everything he can. I think we would miss him if he were gone as he has just fit in here so well in such a short time."

Ruth was happy to be able to have this conversation with her mother. It was so hard doing it on the phone, as they were never able to talk for long because of the cost with the call being long distance. Plus there always seemed to be someone around so she was careful what she said. It would be nice having her mother here for a short visit.

"Why don't we go inside, Mom," Ruth said. I have supper in the oven and I'm sure the children will be back soon.

"Alright, what can I do to help?" was her mother's response. "I came here to help you, now that you have your hands full with the baby. I'll put myself to use and at least set the table.

They both went inside and started to get everything ready for supper. It didn't take long and Billy appeared again running back from next door, this time with Martha running right behind him. Rachel was quite a ways back as her little legs couldn't run as fast. Billy had spilled the news about Ruth's mother being here and the girls couldn't get home fast enough.

Samuel had driven the truck to the shed and was covering the back with a canvas so nothing would get into it easily until he was ready to drive the corn out to the field for planting. It would be far too easy for little critters to find their way into the sacks without a little deterrent. Ruth also knew it wouldn't take him that long and he would be ready to eat. The day's activities would certainly have helped to build his appetite. She was so happy he got home in time and they could now eat together.

When the children reached the house they all ran up the porch steps, as if they were in a race. Billy got inside first and when he got there he stopped when he saw Ruth and her mother standing there looking at him. He was frozen in his steps not knowing what to do. On the other hand, Martha raced in next and ran right past him over to her Grandmother. She grabbed her grandmother by her waist and hung on tight. Mrs. Becker patted her on her back while chuckling at how hard Martha was holding on.

By now Rachel entered the kitchen and also ran over to Ruth's mother grabbing her right leg, as she couldn't quite reach her waste. Mrs. Becker chuckled at how both girls were hanging on to her as tight as they could. She finally got them to loosen their grip and she sat down in one of the kitchen chairs. By doing that Rachel started to climb on her lap. She picked her up and Rachel hugged her around her neck. Martha was standing close as Mrs. Becker put her arm around Martha's waste pulling her close.

Mrs. Becker then said, "Oh my goodness, it's so nice to see you girls. I knew I had to come out here to Greenville and see how you are doing. Have you been enjoying the summer off from school?"

"I don't go to school," Rachel answered.

"I know you don't," acknowledged Mrs. Becker.

"I go to school Grandma," Martha injected. "I am having fun playing. Today Grandpa Schultz played cards with us. Would you play card too?"

"Not right now, my dear," was Mrs. Becker's reply, "I need to help your mother since she has the new baby to take care of."

Martha nodded her head in agreement, knowing how attentive Ruth had been to the new baby all day.

Ruth looked at Billy and asked if Grandpa and Grandma Schultz were coming over for supper. He told her they said 'no' that Grandma Schultz had a ham in the oven and they would be eating that. She then started to set the table adding the extra place for her mother. Had the older Schultzes been joining them she would have set the table in the dining room as it was larger and would better accommodate more people. The kitchen table was right for six without having to add another leaf.

She placed each plate down carefully in front of each chair. She didn't have time to make fresh bread. She hoped what was left in the pantry would be enough for everyone.

Her mother was now helping get things ready. She was dishing out strawberry sauce into small bowls for dessert. Ruth had taken the strawberries out of the freezer earlier that day and they were now thawed out and ready to eat. Their supply was running a little lower with each container they removed. Soon it would be picking season and Ruth would restock the freezer with fresh fruits and vegetables to last another year. They depend on their freezer to keep all of the food they process instead of buying it all at the grocery store. This is country living at its best.

Supper was a happy time. The girls couldn't stop chattering and bringing their Grandma up to speed with everything they did since they saw her last. She just chucked at their enthusiasm. Samuel explained how he and Billy ended up at Ruth's mother's house and how he had forgotten the order list for chickens at home. He also explained how Albert had given him many more sacks of corn than he had expected so it took him much longer than anticipated. It was an eventful day for everyone.

Samuel then looked at Billy and said, "Billy was quite a helper for me today. He was right there when I needed him. He did what he was told. And, he smiled and said thank you to every customer. I think he was a particular hit with Mrs. Gregory who was very curious about who he was and what he was doing with me."

Billy remembered Mrs. Gregory. She was the one who wanted to know if he was leaving in a week. That upset him so. Mr. Schultz had no idea how that upset him. But, he got through it and had tried hard to be a good helper on the route. It was nice to hear Mr. Schultz share his appreciation. It made Billy feel good.

In the past week he had times when he felt bad but many more times when he felt good. It was okay being here with the Schultz family, they treated him well. Maybe he would postpone leaving on his personal journey for a while.

CHAPTER 21

The next morning everyone woke up to the smell of bread baking. Ruth's mother was up exceptionally early and began baking. She loved to bake, especially when there was a need and people would really appreciate it. She noticed that Ruth had placed the last bread from the pantry on the supper table the night before and it soon was all gone. When she made bread she always made extra dough in order to make coffee cake as a special treat. She had the bread and coffee cake in the oven baking and was now mixing up a cake. As long as the oven was hot she thought she might as well make use of it. She knew they'd all like her German chocolate cake; it was one of her specialties.

Soon she had the cake ready for the oven. The bread was now baked and she exchanged it in the oven for the cake. Since she made fresh bread she would make some scrambled eggs for when everyone got up, which she assumed would be soon. Samuel got up earlier and was already in the barn milking. Ruth was up at different times through the night with the baby so she was sleeping a little later than usual this morning.

Mrs. Becker found a chunk of ham in the refrigerator and decided to cut it up and put it with her scrambled eggs. It would be a real feast this morning with the ham and eggs, fresh bread and coffee cake.

When Ruth woke to the smell of freshly baked bread she knew immediately who made it. Before she got up she took the time to say a prayer.

"Dear Heavenly Father, in the past week we have experienced so many blessings. We had no idea what to expect. I am so thankful that you have placed these children in our care. We don't deserve all of the things you do for us but I thank you dear Lord that you show your love for us in our lives in spite of us not deserving it. Please be with Martha, Rachel, Billy and David today. Keep them safe and help them to be happy and stay the joyful children they are. Thank you for bringing my mother to help during a time when I personally need it. Be with Samuel. Keep him safe. Help him to find satisfaction in his work. And, I thank you especially for sending Jesus to be my Savior, which gives me the hope I need to endure the trials and hardships of this life. I owe you everything. Help me to be a good mother, wife and above all a good witness for you. Guide both Samuel and me to be good foster parents. I am sometimes emotionally weak so, please give me strength to get through this day and be with me when the time comes to give up little David. I ask this all in Jesus name. Amen".

She then got up and looked in on Baby David who was still sleeping. She had been up with him around midnight and three o'clock and again at five o'clock, just before Samuel got up. He was sleeping now, which allowed her a chance to get dressed and ready for a new day. When she was finished dressing she carefully picked up Baby David, making sure not to wake him, and headed downstairs. As she reached the kitchen she could see her mother standing by the stove frying up the eggs she had mixed together. It brought comfort to Ruth to see her mother standing there with her old apron she had when Ruth was still living at home on their homestead. Right now she so appreciated the comfort and security of having her mother there. She didn't understand why, as she felt very secure with Samuel too. It just felt good and she was overwhelmed with gratitude to God for bringing her mother to her.

"Good morning" Ruth said as she walked toward her mother. "You've been busy this morning. You must have been up very early. Did you sleep much last night?"

Her mother looked at her and said, "I got up with Samuel. I heard him walk down the steps and then I got up and came down here. I did hear little David a couple times overnight but I went right back to sleep again. I always sleep better in the country."

Ruth got the basket from the living room and put Baby David down so she could help her mother. Then she realized breakfast was made and there wasn't anything for her to do. So, she got Baby David's bottle ready, as when he woke up this time he'd be looking for it.

It didn't take long and Samuel was on his way in from the barn, the children were all stirring upstairs and Baby David was awake crying for his bottle. Ruth started to feed David and her mother headed upstairs to help the children. This was the start of a day that would repeat itself throughout the week. Soon it would be Friday, the day that Mrs. Adams would come back to take Baby David to his new parents. Ruth was starting to fear that day and knew it would be here soon. Her attachment to Baby David was getting stronger and stronger, something everyone was afraid would happen and did.

The day flew by. Samuel took the pickup truck to the new field and parked it there as he walked home to get the tractor and planting equipment. He was now able to start the process of planting his new ten acres, something he had been planning all winter long.

He had no trouble picking out the good seed from the bad in the sacks Albert gave him. The damage was on the bottom of each sack, as they got wet. The leak in Albert's roof must have been at one end of Albert's feed storage shed and the water then ran across the floor, damaging the bottom of the sacks of feed. It would have done more damage if the leak was right above the inventory.

Samuel estimated that he would be able to use at least eighty percent of each bag. He simply scooped out the good corn seed and left the bad seed in the damaged sacks. He'd figure out what to do with the rotting seed later. Right now he just wanted to get the field planted.

~⁕~

Grandma Becker entertained Martha and Rachel in the kitchen. She made a day of baking everything she could. The girls were happy to help bake cookies. By the time they were done they had flour and sugar in their hair and all over the front of their clothes. It didn't matter as they had so much fun.

The kitchen was full of chatter all day long. It was just what the girls needed so they wouldn't focus on how Baby David was taking their mother's attention away from them. Ruth's mother was very happy with the situation. She was needed, she wasn't alone and she was doing things she thoroughly enjoyed. Everything seemed to be working out for everyone.

~⁕~

Billy was on his own as everyone was preoccupied. No one seemed to notice him step outside to play with Terry. He saw how the baby was taking all of Ruth's attention. He knew Samuel was busy in the field and didn't need him. And, Martha and Rachel were totally absorbed with their other Grandma.

He wondered if his own Grandmother would ever show love toward him like Martha and Rachel's Grandparents did to them. He knew that was probably not possible, as he hadn't heard from or about her for years. Clearly she didn't want him. Mrs. Adams said she contacted her after his father got taken away. By now surely he would have heard from her. He knew he would never understand why she didn't want any part of him. He asked himself one more time what had he done to deserve that?

Just then he heard Ruth call to him, "Billy, would you be so kind as to feed the chickens? The feed is in the feed shed in the covered barrels.

You will find the scoop hanging on a nail right next to them and there is a bucket to use standing next to the barrel."

"Okay," Bill said and started walking toward the feed shed.

He hadn't done it alone before but after the egg route experience he was willing to try. He actually didn't do too badly. He found the feed in the feed shed and filled the bucket about half full. He couldn't carry any more and would just make a couple of trips. He went in the chicken yard and dumped the chicken feed in the feeders. The chickens were right there starting to eat as he dumped the food. He thought he must have done it right or they wouldn't be so anxious to eat it.

When he was done feeding the chickens he headed for the grove behind the barn with Terry, his beloved friend. There he would play catch with Terry and then lie on the ground and look up at the sky. Terry would lie next to him. Their bond kept growing. It would be so hard for him to leave Terry behind when he finally had to leave.

He was growing fond of the farm as well. He was starting to wonder if leaving on one of his adventures would be the right thing. Just being here was an adventure in itself. Just then he realized how he had been waffling back and forth on whether to leave on his personal adventure or stay here with the Schultzes. He wondered why he kept changing his mind. It probably was because of the uncertainly in not knowing if he really could stay and he didn't want to be taken away before he could run away. He'd just have to keep thinking about it and be ready for a last minute exit, if needed.

He could hear Samuel's tractor in the background. The new field was just over the hill from the grove. He wondered if it would be okay for him to walk to the field. If anyone at the house needed him they surely would guess that he would be in the grove and maybe even the field. He'd take his chances.

As he got over the hill he could see Samuel on his tractor with the corn planter behind it. He walked carefully toward where Samuel was planting. Samuel saw him coming and he waved Billy over to the truck.

When he was done with the row he was planting he got off the tractor and walked over to the truck.

He had a scowl on his face when he said, "Billy, why are you here? Does Mom know you walked out here?"

Billy hung his head, as he knew he shouldn't have left the farmyard without telling someone. "No, I didn't tell anyone. They are all so busy."

Samuel said in a firm voice, "Don't you do that again. It's almost lunchtime so I'll take you back with me. I'm going to drive the pickup back and remove some of these bad seed bags. I need to make room on the truck to move the sacks around."

His scolding turned into a conversation where he shared what he was doing with Billy. He was now speaking with him like a partner in his work.

"I need to pick up my tool box. I didn't have room for it with all of the seed sacks. I think I need to tighten a bolt on the corn planter." Then he added, "Ruth will be worried about you."

Billy spoke and said, "She is so busy with the baby she didn't know I left the yard. She asked me to feed the chickens, which I did. I then went to the grove to play. She never comes out there."

Samuel said, "It doesn't matter, you still need to let her know."

"Alright" was Billy's answer. He wasn't going to argue, as he didn't want to upset Samuel. This was the first scolding he got from Samuel, although it really wasn't too bad. He knew that Samuel cared for him or he wouldn't be so concerned. In an odd way, that sort of made him feel good.

CHAPTER 22

The week went by quickly. Finally, that infamous day arrived. It was Friday and Mrs. Adams would be there around ten o'clock. It seemed like a normal day but Ruth knew it was not. She was up early standing over Baby David's crib just watching him. He was a happy baby always ready to give a smile when someone cared for him. This morning he was especially happy. It was almost like he knew his new parents were in town ready to take him.

Everyone else was already downstairs eating breakfast. Ruth found it difficult to take Baby David downstairs, as it would be the first phase of his departure. Finally she forced herself to make the move to gather his belongings, pick him up and go downstairs. She knew everyone was worried about her as she was inseparable from the baby all week long. It was just the thing that Samuel expressed concern over when they decided to take the baby into their home. Yes, it would be difficult for her but somehow she would get through it. She had prayed for the Lord to give her strength and she just had to trust that he would pull her through.

When she got downstairs breakfast was over and it was quiet. Everyone knew the baby would be leaving and there was sadness in the house. That is everyone except Baby David. He was giggling and pumping his arms and legs up and down when anyone would come close to the basket in which Ruth put him. Maybe he enjoyed the extra attention he was getting. Maybe he just knew his new parents were waiting for his arrival.

It was time. Mrs. Adams' car was coming down the driveway. Soon Baby David would be gone. She stopped in her normal spot right in front of the back porch door, got out of her car and started walking toward the house. She was met by Martha and Billy.

Martha was the first to speak, "Are you here to take David away?"

She was startled, "David? Where did that name come from?"

Martha was more than happy to give the answer, not knowing the name was going to be their secret, "That's what Mommy named him. We all call him Baby David. Mommy says he's a giant killer and needed the name David, like David in the Bible."

Mrs. Adams didn't know what to do with this information. She thought she might just keep it to herself and see what happens.

She decided to speak with Billy since he was standing there taking this all in, "Billy, is everything still okay with you?"

This time he was quick to answer, "Yes, Mrs. Adams. I got to go on the egg route, feed the chickens and watch Mr. Schultz plant corn."

Mrs. Adams smiled and said, "It sounds like you have had a busy week. It also sounds like you are enjoying yourself. You'll have to tell me all about it when I come back in a couple of weeks."

Billy nodded in agreement. She could see a real change in him. Could it be that he was starting to come out of his shell? That would be a lot in just a short time. It was the miracle she was hoping for.

She started one more time for the porch steps. She didn't like this part of her job. The good part was giving children to parents who wanted them and would provide a great home for them. The bad part was taking them away from their families and, in this case, taking them from foster parents who have become attached. She knew from her phone conversations that Ruth had gotten attached and it would be hard for her to give up the child.

She headed up the steps with Martha at her heels. Billy decided to stay outside and play on the tree swing for a while. He wasn't too anxious to see the other foster child, he shared the house with, get taken away.

Rachel was sitting by Ruth's side waiting for her turn to get her mother's attention. Ruth was holding Baby David. The basket was on the kitchen table ready for Mrs. Adams to use to put Baby David in when she took him. Not much came with this new baby when Mrs. Adams brought him to the farm so there wasn't much going back with him.

Ruth's mother had retreated to the living room to do a little reading. It was apparent she didn't think it was her place to be there when Mrs. Adams arrived. It would be hard for Ruth to give up the baby and it was good her mother would be there for her.

Ruth had a hard time putting Baby David in the basket again. Mrs. Adams patiently waited for her to make the move and didn't want to pressure her. Finally, Ruth did place the baby in the basket and then took a step back to catch her breath.

Samuel walked over to her side and put his arm around her shoulder. He wanted to offer comfort. Rachel was hanging on to her reaching up to her waist wanting her attention. Ruth put her hand on Rachel's head to hold her down from trying to climb up. The touch seemed to settle Rachel down.

Mrs. Adams thanked Ruth and Samuel and then walked out the door with the basket in hand. It all happened so quickly. Mrs. Adams seemed to know that moving quickly would avoid any unnecessary lingering good-byes. This would be the last time the Schultzes would see Baby David and best it is over quickly. Ruth stood there in silent without any emotion on her face. She appeared to be in a daze.

You could hear a car door slam. Soon the sound of the car engine was the only sound as it was completely silent in the house. Then you could hear the sound of the tires traveling slowly over the gravel driveway as they cleared the turn around the windmill and then went faster as the car past the house and headed to the highway. Shortly you couldn't hear the sounds of Mrs. Adams car at all. There was complete silence both inside and outside. It was over.

Samuel looked at Ruth with great concern wondering what would happen next. Ruth then excused herself and walked up the stairs to their bedroom. He knew that his greatest fear had come true in that Ruth became so attached to the baby that she was now overcome with a sense of hopelessness.

Rachel looked up at him and said, "Where is Mommy going?"

Trying to avoid the question He looked at Martha and Rachel and said, "Why don't you both go outside and play with Billy on the swings or in the sandbox. We'll call you in when lunch is ready."

They both looked a little sad as they sensed their mother was upset. Knowing there was nothing they could do they complied and went outside to play.

Samuel looked into the living room at Ruth's mother. Their eye contact spoke volumes. Without speaking a word they both knew their worst fear had indeed come true. They would now just have to wait and see the outcome.

Mrs. Becker went into the kitchen and started to make lunch. It would soon be time to eat. Plus, this action would give her something to do in what was a very uncomfortable situation.

Samuel decided to leave Ruth alone for a while. He would go upstairs and check on her when lunch was ready. He retreated to the living room and sat down on the couch in the exact place Ruth's mother had vacated earlier.

As he sat there he lower his head and said a silent prayer, "O God, please help Ruth. Don't let this take her down. Give her the strength she needs to get through this. Amen."

There it was, short and to the point. He knew that God would know what was on his mind and God would know what to do. He just sat there feeling powerless hoping God would step in soon.

In a while Mrs. Becker stood in the living room door and told Samuel lunch would be ready soon and maybe he should go upstairs and check on Ruth. He knew he needed to do that but wasn't looking forward to it. He got up and slowly began the walk to their bedroom. When he got there he knocked and when he didn't get an answer he opened the door slowly and looked in. He saw Ruth sitting on the bed with a handkerchief in her hand. She had been crying. She just sat there staring out the window in silence.

Samuel walked over to the bed and sat down next to Ruth. Much to his surprise she spoke first.

"Samuel, I have been sitting here crying as it really hurt me to give up Baby David. It brought back too many memories that I had put away for a long time. I don't want to feel that hurt again. I know you are concerned about me. I know that Mom is concerned as well. I've had a few days to prepare for this but nothing could prepare me for how I felt when Mrs. Adams walked out the door with David."

Samuel started to say something and she interrupted him, "Let me finish, I need to say this."

He leaned back and let Ruth speak, "When Mrs. Adams called and said she had a baby I was really excited as I thought in having a baby it would give me some fulfillment that I thought I needed. Now that the baby is gone I don't feel the type of fulfillment I was looking for. All I feel is helpless and sad. I feel like I neglected the rest of my family during this week, as I was so preoccupied with caring for the baby. That was selfish of me. I don't want to be a neglectful wife and mother. I overlooked how fulfilled I really do feel as your wife and mother to our children. I feel like I cheated you and the girls and we lost a week of precious time. I don't want to do that again."

Samuel reached out and touched Ruth's hand. He carefully picked her hand up and brought it to his face where he kissed it tenderly and then held it with both hands against his chest. She watched this act of affection, as it wasn't often that Samuel showed his emotions in this way. It just reaffirmed his love for her and she loved him even more now than ever.

Ruth turned and looked right into Samuel's eyes and said, "Samuel, thank you for being here for me and understanding what I am going through. I love that about you and I feel so blessed to have you as my husband."

All Samuel could do was smile back at her as words were not his forte and Ruth knew it. She was content with his acts of kindness and the special looks he gave her that displayed more than words could ever express. If she had to pick one she would pick the actions that reinforced their love rather than words that might not be real.

Ruth had one more thing to say so she continued their conversation, "I love the idea of taking in foster children. I really think this is what God has in mind for us to do. Having Billy with us has added something special to our family. I had a moment with Billy earlier this week that made me feel like I was really helping him. I have seen a change in him since he came here and that's what I want us to do with these children they bring to us. He is a very special young boy. I've been thinking about this a lot over the past few weeks and I think giving up Billy would be unbearable. I was able to give up Baby David because I knew when he came I would have to. Although I also know Billy could be leaving us, I really don't want that to happen. Samuel, do you feel the same way?"

Samuel seemed moved by her comments. His response was quick and to the point, "Ruth, I have been so happy with Billy and I too have wanted to bring up the topic but didn't know how. Since you have asked me, I would love nothing better than if he stayed with us forever."

"Do you really mean that?" Ruth was astonished at his comment. Could they have been thinking the same thing about Billy? She continued, "I didn't want to say anything as I thought it was too soon to know for certain."

Samuel took the moment and went right to the point again, "Would you like to adopt Billy and make him ours?"

"Oh yes, that would make me very, very happy, Samuel. Do you think that would be possible?"

"I think it certainly would be possible. He fits right in and unless you knew differently you would think he was ours from the start. I know that God works in many different ways and maybe all of the events since we decided to take in foster children are his way of bringing Billy to us."

"Samuel, I couldn't agree more. Do you think Martha and Rachel will like the idea?"

"I have been watching them with Billy and I have to say that they all are so good together. It really does seem like we are all one family. I think it would seem like a natural thing to keep him with the girls and us. They might like the idea of having a permanent big brother."

Ruth got a very concerned look on her face as she added one more important issue, "What do you think Billy will think of this? He is so confused about how he has been tossed around. He has never understood the rejection from both his father and grandmother."

"I've been thinking about that as well," Samuel said. "I believe the only way we will find the answer is to simply ask him. It would have to be at the right moment, so we don't get rejected by him, which is certainly possible."

"I agree," Ruth responded. "We don't have to do this right away. I do want it to be the right time. I think you and I will know when that is. I'm not even sure we should say anything to Mrs. Adams until we are really ready or she might force the issue and that will only confuse Billy. She has already hinted at it several times when she has talked with me so I think she would be in total favor of us doing this."

"Agreed," Samuel said while he nodded his head in total agreement.

Ruth wiped her eyes to remove any last tears that had collected during this serious conversation about these life-changing matters. She was now ready to go downstairs and get things back to normal. She started to get up and then sat down again.

"Samuel, giving up Baby David was very difficult for me. I didn't think it would be but it was. I don't think we should take babies any more. I want our girls to be our babies and I don't want to replace them with any others. Would you be okay with that?"

Samuel sat there for a moment gathering his thoughts before he spoke. "I knew it would be hard on you when you would have to give up the baby. Yet, I never expected to hear what you just told me. Yes, I will support you. There are many older children in need of foster homes too, maybe even more than there are babies who are in much higher demand to be adopted. We just need to call Mrs. Adams and tell her. I'm certain she will respect our wishes. She knows about us losing babies. And, she loves having us as foster parents."

Relief came across Ruth's face. Samuel made it so simple. Why had she worried about telling him her concerns? This was an answer to prayers. At that moment Samuel grabbed his wife and held her close. They sat there for a couple of minutes saying nothing just holding each other tightly.

After the couple of minutes were up and Samuel loosened his hold a bit, Ruth said, "Let's go downstairs and have lunch with our children?"

She smiled, put her handkerchief back in her apron pocket and got up. She reached for Samuel's hand. He too got up and together they went hand in hand downstairs.

When they reached the kitchen Ruth gave her mother a big smile and said, "Mom, I am so happy you have been here for all of us. This week would have been difficult without your help. Thank you so much from the bottom of my heart."

Ruth's mother was surprised as she expected to see a dejected Ruth, not one with a smile and kind words of thanks. This was truly a great turn of events. Her mother looked over to Samuel who just smiled and nodded his head as to say 'yes you heard right, Ruth is all right, everything is back to normal'.

Ruth then went outside and called for the children. She stood at the bottom of the porch steps as they ran towards her. She hugged each of the girls who were quick to grab her. She then reached out and pulled Billy toward her as well so he too could enjoy the feeling of being loved and wanted. She knew her place and where she would be able to give the most. She loved these children, all three of them, and didn't want to miss anything or mess anything up in the process of their growing up. With the children all still hanging on to her and she to them, they all went inside and had lunch together as a family.

CHAPTER 23

Life around the Schultz farm got back to normal quickly. It was Sunday and the whole family just attended worship and Sunday School and were on their way back home. Even Ruth's mother was still with them as she decided to stay until Tuesday when she would go back to the city with Ruth and Samuel on the egg route. Gerhard and Anna were both well and enjoyed their Sunday worship, something very dear to them.

Everyone was looking forward to a treasured Sunday afternoon that would be filled with family activities. They enjoyed one another and the Sunday afternoons together helped to bond them as a family and build their appreciation for each other. Sundays were respected as the Lord's Day and unless there was an emergency seldom did Samuel work in the field.

It was a full car with Samuel and Ruth in the front seat with Billy in the middle. In the back seat Martha sat between Samuel's parents, while Rachel sat on Grandma Becker's lap. It was a tight fit but no one seemed to care.

The children were buzzing about Sunday School, including Billy. They had a guest speaker that preached in worship and also came to the Sunday School opening. He had just gotten back from South America on a missionary trip and had lots to tell. The excitement of the adventure caught Billy's attention. It was just his kind of talk. Each Sunday got a little more exciting for him and he was now looking forward to the next one.

Once they got home, everyone headed for the house, as they knew dinner wouldn't be long. Ruth often put it in the oven while they were in church so when they got home it would be ready. The smell of the beef roast was very inviting as the whole crew entered the house single file. Once inside all of the adults took on a task and things got ready quickly.

Dinner was served in the dining room where they all fit around the dining room table. Ruth's roast included potatoes, carrots, celery and onions, all roasted together in the oven, making quite a feast. Her mother made a beautiful angel food cake with blueberry sauce to drizzle over it. She whipped up some cream to add a delicious topping completing her masterpiece. All in all, everyone enjoyed Sunday dinner.

After dinner it was time for relaxation, as soon as the dishes were done. In the meantime the men went off to the front porch to read the paper, or take a nap, whichever came first. The children played quietly coloring on the dining room table that they took over as soon as it had been cleared. The women joined the task of washing dishes. Since there were three of them it went quickly.

When they were done they took off to the living room to chat and do some handwork. The two grandmothers worked on some crocheting while Ruth was darning socks that needed mending. It was all peaceful and exceptionally quiet.

Ruth looked up a few times to watch the children. The girls were coloring intensely. Billy wasn't quite as occupied. He kept looking out the window and looked less content. Ruth got an idea.

She put down her darning and said, "Billy, I think it's time to take a look in that attic and see what we can find to decorate your room. What do you think?"

He turned and gave her a gigantic grin saying, "Oh yes that would be great."

Ruth then got up and said, "Let's go!"

"Can we come too," was the chant from Martha and Rachel.

"Of course you can, we'll make a treasure hunt out of this." Ruth then called to Samuel, "Samuel, do you want to join us? We might need some help lifting some boxes in the attic."

"Sure," was the response from the front porch as he was close enough to hear the conversation!

Soon Samuel came through the front door as the children and Ruth waited for him.

Ruth then said to everyone, "I think we should change out of our Sunday clothes as it will be dirty in the attic. I'll meet you all at the attic door in five minutes. Let's go."

By saying that, a race ensued and everyone hurried toward the steps trying to get there first, including Samuel and Ruth. The children all thought it was funny that both Samuel and Ruth joined in the unofficial race. Samuel picked up Rachel as she struggled to keep up because she was giggling so much. Ruth grabbed Billy and slowed him down giving Martha a chance to catch up. Even Billy found humor in being held back as he kept trying to get ahead. There wasn't an official winner as Martha and Billy reached the top together. Clearly everyone was having a good time at the start of this Schultz family treasure hunt.

⁕⁂⁕

The children were very timely and even beat the five-minute deadline. Billy was the first to reach the door and stood there like a soldier watching guard until all of the others would arrive.

While they were changing clothes Ruth and Samuel just smiled at each other.

Samuel finally said, "This is what I want in our lives, to bring happiness to the children, doing things that make us happy too.

"Yes, and all of this after spending the morning in the Lord's house," Ruth added. "What more could we ask?"

"I agree," was Samuel's response along with, "We'd better hurry or the kids are going to beat us again."

When Samuel and Ruth got to the attic door all of the children were standing there with suspicious smiles on their faces, ready for the next event. None of them were going to be caught off guard if something like the race they just had was to start again.

Samuel opened the door and led the way upstairs. He knew there were some boxes in the path that needed to be moved so they had a place to stand when they got up there. After he did that, everyone scattered and found a place to start their search.

The Wagner families had left a lot of things in the attic when they moved out because they didn't have a place to store them in their retirement homes. They told Samuel and Ruth that they could either use the stuff or get rid of it, as they wouldn't be coming back for it. Ruth and Samuel didn't even know what was up there so this truly was a treasure hunt.

There was a box marked 'porcelain animals' that caught Martha's attention. Samuel helped open the box for Martha and Rachel. They did their usual thing and giggled while they unpacked the contents.

"Mommy, can we put these on our dresser?" Martha asked.

Ruth looked up and saw the small porcelain dog Martha was holding and said, "I think you can but, why don't you and Rachel pick two each. Maybe we can put one on your dresser and the other in the china cabinet. I think that will be enough to start with."

Ruth knew that if she didn't limit their find they would want the whole box and that would be too much for now. Focusing on their choice would keep them busy for sometime, as they loved all the porcelain animals in the box.

Looking over at Samuel, Ruth could see that he found a couple of old chairs that he was looking over to see how much repair they needed. She was thinking that maybe he could use them in the living room now that they have one more person when they watched television. They could also be brought into the kitchen when they had a bigger group to serve.

Ruth too was looking through some boxes filled with old curtains and curtain rods. She wondered where they had been and if they were good enough to use again to update their house. They never had a lot of money so the curtains they used were curtains she made from some leftover material her mother had given her along with some make shift bed sheets as liners. She would be happy if these curtains fit the windows. They might be a little frayed but she and her mother could fix that.

Billy quietly found a pot of gold. He opened a box and there was a stack of old magazines. In fact, they were National Geographic magazines bursting with pictures of far-away places. He couldn't believe it. How could he have been so lucky to find this one box filled with so much adventure?

The first one he picked up was dated January 1939. He was browsing through it and saw an article about Long Island, New York with a map of New York City. It pinpointed the Statue of Liberty and the Empire State Building. His curiosity was peaked thinking about all of the sites in just one location.

There was another article about the Cape Horn Ship Race. Men were climbing up a huge pole to work on the sails of a huge sailboat, while waves were coming over the ship's deck. It looked so exciting. These magazines were much better than the ones he brought with him in his pillowcase.

As Billy continued his adventure through the magazine he saw an article on Peru. There was an aerial view of the landing field in Lima. Then there was a picture of a marketplace where a woman was sitting on the ground handing out bread to people and another one handing over a live chicken to someone who must be buying it.

He saw a group of men with skirts on top of their trousers with a caption saying they were in their native costumes. Billy wondered where this place called Peru was in South America. Was it near the place the missionary at church had been? He was getting more and more excited as he continued to flip through the pages.

Here he had a whole box full of adventure. There had to be at least two dozen National Geographic magazines. How could he be so lucky to be the one to find them? They were perfect. How would he ever take them all with him when he had to leave? The box was so heavy.

Standing next to the box was an old magazine rack that would hold many of his new magazines as well as his personal collection. He was ecstatic and he hadn't even found something to hang on his wall yet. He was clearly having a lot of fun and was so happy that he could be part of this great treasure hunt.

⁓

Samuel put down his chairs thinking he would come up and get them sometime, when he had time to work on them. He walked over to Martha and Rachel and told them to be careful, as they were getting a little careless with the porcelain statues. The statues had been wrapped in newspaper, which was now strewn all over the floor around each of them.

"Maybe you have unwrapped enough to find what you need," Samuel suggested. "Why don't you pick the ones you want and then start wrapping the others up again and put them back in their box? Do you need some help?"

"No Daddy" Martha said with Rachel repeating her words, "No Daddy."

Samuel then saw Ruth unfolding her curtains, which were a little heavy. He came to her rescue and helped unfold each panel and fold them up again when they passed inspection. They actually were in good shape.

Ruth said, "These curtains are wonderful. I'm going to take them down with us. Maybe our mothers will help me fix any torn areas, after we check to see if they will fit the windows. I'll wash them tomorrow when I get done with our clothes. If they hang on the line that will perk them up a little and make them very inviting for our windows. I am so excited to have them. Look, there are also curtain rods as well."

Samuel checked out the rods and said, "If the curtains fit the windows I'll have Dad help me and we will mount the rods so you can hang the curtains after you wash them. There weren't any rods on the windows when we came. It looked like there had been some."

Ruth said, "Remember, Marie Wagner said they took the rods for their new house because they were new and they needed them. That's why we made our own curtain rods out of wooden dowels. If these were the ones they took down when they got new ones they should fit the windows. I don't care if they are a little worn, they will be much better than the make shift ones we have. This is a real find Samuel."

"Thanks for coming up with the idea. I think the children are really enjoying this activity," Samuel inserted. "I found a couple of chairs that need just a little repair and I know we can use them. Between the chairs and the curtains we might have saved ourselves a bit of money too."

So far, the attic full of the unknown treasures was a great idea and made the day a great family adventure.

CHAPTER 24

The attic treasure hunt went on for about an hour. Billy was happy with his magazines and magazine rack, that he found earlier, but he still didn't find anything for his bedroom walls.

Ruth spoke up and said to everyone in the attic, "I think we've looked enough, let's start getting ready to take what we found and go downstairs."

The girls started to put their discarded statues back in the box in which they found them, while Samuel and Ruth packed up the curtains Ruth had been looking through. Billy didn't stop his search and it was clear he would continue until the last minute and he was told to stop.

A little more time passed when all of a sudden Billy shouted out, "Wow, this is great!"

It startled everyone who stopped what they were doing and looked in Billy's direction.

"What did you find?" Samuel asked.

"Look at this," Billy said while pointing to a piece of carpeting he had partially unrolled on the floor.

Everyone came to where Billy was. On the floor was a partially unrolled hooked carpet that had the most beautiful picture of what looked to be a western rodeo.

The carpet carried a detailed design of a cowboy riding a bucking horse with a stand full of people watching. There were a few more cowboys sitting on top of the fence with still others on horses ready to rescue the rider at the end of his ride. The cowboy on the bronco was waving his right arm in the air to keep his balance, while hanging on tightly to a rope wrapped around his left hand. You could almost imagine the battle between the cowboy and the horse as the picture revealed the horse dropping his head toward the ground while kicking his back legs out as far as possible trying to unseat the rider. What a scene Billy found in this hooked carpet masterpiece.

Samuel helped Billy unroll the rest of the carpet to see a far off mountain with a stream and trees making it a complete and perfect scene. The hooked rug was done in great detail with many vivid, rich colors that still looked like new.

"I don't believe I have ever seen a carpet hanging on a wall before," Ruth said.

Billy's smile instantly turned into a frown displaying his disappointment after his great find.

Ruth then continued, "Billy, I think you can do what you want, it is your room and it is a fine-looking piece of art. I'm sure Samuel can find a way to hang it up. It might fit perfectly on the wall right across from your bed. What do you think Samuel?"

As she turned to look at Samuel he wasn't there. She then heard him from across the attic.

"I found these hooks over here earlier. I think I can mount them on the wall. Then we can fashion some wire or something to the rug and hang it over these hooks. I think we can make it work."

Billy was smiling again a smile that was the biggest he had displayed since he got to the Schultz farm. It was clear that the afternoon in the attic had taken his mind off his personal matters and brought some happiness that now was displayed on his face.

Ruth raised her arms and pointed to the steps and said, "Okay then, let's go and hang it up".

She picked up some of the statues the girls couldn't carry while Samuel said, "I'll come back up later and bring the curtains down."

They were now all heading to the second floor to the bedrooms. Samuel carried the carpet and Billy had his arms full of magazines plus he was hanging on to the magazine rack. He was overloaded and could only take about eight magazines. He thought he would come back later to get the rest, as he had no intention of leaving such a great find in the attic.

When Billy got to his room he went in and walked right over to the window. He put down the magazine rack and put the National Geographic stack on one side. He then went over to his dresser, pulled open the top draw and took out his tattered magazines he brought with him. Without pausing a second, he walked over to the magazine rack and put them on the other side of the rack. Then he stepped back and simply admired his new find.

Samuel laid down the rug in the hallway and went back upstairs to get the hooks he left behind. Ruth was in with the girls cleaning off the top of their dresser to make room for their new statues. They were all excited and chattering busily.

Billy was sitting on his bed waiting for Samuel and admiring his new magazine rack filled with colorful magazines thinking about the many great adventures he would have looking through them.

Just then Samuel was in his doorway with hooks and a folded up ruler in one hand and a hammer in the other.

"Let's get this done Billy so we can hang that rug."

Billy nodded in agreement.

"Billy, you hold the ruler to the floor, I want to measure where I put the hooks. I measured the carpet in the hallway so I need to measure the height of the wall so we can center it."

Billy and Samuel were working diligently at measuring the wall to get it just right. By now Ruth and the girls were standing in the doorway watching this labor of love. Ruth then said she was going downstairs to find something to attach to the back of the rug that would allow them to hang it over the hooks. When she left the girls sat down in the doorway watching intently at what their Dad and Billy were doing.

It didn't take long and she was back with some wire. All of the grandparents were right behind her having heard about the project when she went downstairs. Everyone was anxious to see Billy's exciting find.

Ruth asked Grandpa Schultz to help her and they went back into the hallway to work on the rug mounting. Together they carefully attached a piece of wire to each edge of the carpet corners at the top so they could loop over the hooks Samuel was now fastening to the wall.

If all of the measuring were accurate, the carpet would fit right under the mounted hooks. Now it was time to mount the carpet to the wall. Samuel and his father picked it up and carried it to its new assigned location. They dropped the corner wires over the hooks and it fit perfectly. It was on the wall right across from Billy's bed so he could look at it while in bed each night.

It was more beautiful than Billy thought once it was on the wall. He couldn't understand how he could find such a thing that was just perfect for him. In the scene he could imagine himself in so many places. He could be riding the stallion or sitting on one of those horses ready to help. He could also just be sitting in the stands cheering on the cowboy. He loved the adventure of it all.

Billy was still starring at the interwoven picture on his wall not realizing everyone was starring at him. Finally he looked around and saw everyone looking at him and was a little embarrassed.

After a few uncomfortable moments Billy turned to Samuel and Ruth and simply said, "Thank you."

He was touched by the events of the afternoon and wanted to let the Schultzes know he really was thankful. He couldn't help but think that these people treated him as if he were part of the family. It made him wonder why his own family couldn't treat him this way. He wasn't a bad person so why did they treat him like he was bad? His mood quickly changed and he was instantly sad again.

Billy could feel a tear forming in his eye and he focused on not letting it run down his face exposing his sensitivity. Sometimes when you try too hard not to cry that's just when you can't stop it. Soon a tear did run down his cheek. He didn't know if anyone had seen it and he quickly brushed it away hoping no one did.

He realized that Ruth must have noticed as she made an effort to clear the room, which Billy really appreciated.

Ruth said, "Okay, I think it's time for a treat. Mom, do you have some of the cookies left you and the girls made this week. I think we should have some with coffee and milk."

"Oh yes," her mother chimed in, "I'll go down and get them ready and put some coffee on the stove."

Now the grandparents, with Martha and Rachel right behind them, headed downstairs.

Billy was back to staring at the picture on his wall when Ruth came over and sat on the bed next to him with Samuel standing by her side.

She looked at Billy and said, "Billy we have been so happy with you being here with us. We want you to know that you are special. You have such a great imagination. You are always so willing to help. And, you are so polite. We want you to feel welcome in our home for as long as you want to be here."

Samuel then added, "I hope the chores I have asked you to do haven't been a burden and you have felt at home with us. I'm happy we found these things in the attic and that you like them in your room."

Billy heard what Ruth said about his being polite so he felt compelled to say something in response to what they were saying to him. His mother had taught him to always say thank you and show his appreciation for things given to him.

"Thank you for the magazines and the carpet for my wall. You have been really good to me."

After a short pause he added more that was on his mind without thinking about how personal it was getting. He just needed to get some things off his mind that had been bothering him. It seemed safe to talk with Ruth and Samuel.

"I miss my Mom but I don't miss my Dad, maybe I should but he doesn't want me. I've never known my grandma but I guess she doesn't want me either."

He paused for a little bit trying to hold back the emotion that was again building within him. His focus turned to an expression of self-pity as he continued, "I try and be good and bad things still happen to me. Why don't people want me? I can't figure it out and I try so hard so I won't say the wrong thing or do something bad."

He looked so sad sitting on the bed next to Ruth, who clearly wanted to ease his pain. For the first time Samuel saw the hurt that Billy was now expressing with his words and the tears that couldn't be held back.

As a few more tears slid down Billy's cheeks, Ruth finally put her arms around him and pulled him close to her. Samuel put his hand on Billy's shoulder trying to console him in some way. Billy just couldn't understand why people didn't want him. He was so hurt by that.

After a little while Billy sat back and again wiped a few tears from his face. Ruth did a now familiar gesture and pulled her handkerchief from her apron pocket and brushed his cheeks carefully to make them dry again.

She then said, "I see that you are hurting and I'm not sure what we can do to make that hurt go away. You are a wonderful boy and I'm sure your mother loved you very much and would not have left you if she could have avoided getting sick."

Billy was looking directly at her, listening to every word. He needed comfort and he was happy to have Mr. and Mrs. Schultz to talk to right now.

Ruth then continued, "Your father and grandmother are missing out seeing a nice young boy grow up. It is truly their loss."

Samuel then added, "In the meantime, you can be with us and be part of our family. Will that be okay with you?"

Billy nodded his head in agreement and there was again a moment of silence. He knew he could stay as long as he was in the welfare program because Mr. and Mrs. Schultz were foster parents and he felt that they did like him so he felt it was safe to agree.

"I mean, Billy, we would like you to be a permanent member of our family," Samuel was trying to make his point clear.

Ruth helped to make sure that Billy totally understood what Samuel just said so she added, "Billy, we want to adopt you. We want to know if that would be okay with you. We want to be your mother and father and Martha and Rachel would be your sisters."

"What do you think Billy?" Samuel tried to get some feedback.

Billy was so shocked that he just stared out the window with his mouth a little open and his eyes wide. Ruth looked up at Samuel with a look of concern. Samuel was looking back at her shaking his head in disappointment. Billy wasn't immediately responding to their offer.

Billy then said, "Why do you want me to be your son? My Dad and grandma didn't want me. I must not be a good person."

Samuel and Ruth had immediate eye contact again. Billy watched them as they looked at each other. He was convinced that they agreed with him and would withdraw their offer. Why did he say that, he probably ruined his chances to stay here and he really did want to stay?

Ruth spoke slowly and carefully in her response, "Billy, I'm going to tell you something and I hope you understand what I am going to say. Over the past few years, while Samuel and I have been married, we have lost three babies who died instead of being born. One of them would be about your age, if he had lived."

Billy frowned at that statement, while still looking out the window, so Ruth added, "Yes, he was a boy. We were so sad we didn't know what to do. We prayed and God came to our rescue and gave us Martha and Rachel. However, the last time we lost a baby we couldn't have another one and that made us wonder if we did something wrong, just like you are thinking you might have done something wrong. Well, we were wrong to think that. Billy, when bad things happen to you it doesn't mean you have done something wrong."

Ruth was getting a little emotional herself so Samuel joined in explaining, "We heard about the foster care program and that's how we got you. We have talked about you and how you fit perfectly with us ever since you got here. We believe that God sent you to us as he wants you with us."

Ruth then took over again, "Billy you have become part of the Schultz family and we would be just as sad if you left as we were when we lost our three children. We do want you to be our son. Won't you please consider becoming a member of our family?"

Finally Billy turned back to the both of them and said, "You really want me as your son?"

"Yes, we most certainly do," Samuel replied.

"Oh yes, Billy, we would love it if you would stay with us forever," Ruth said with a tender smile.

In a meek manner and a soft voice Billy gave his answer, "I really would like it if you were my Mom and Dad. I like being here." You could see just a sliver of a smile forming at each corner of his mouth when he asked, "Is it really true, can I call you Mom and Dad?"

Ruth and Samuel both caught their breath, as they didn't realize that would be a question.

"Well son, you certainly can call me Dad," Samuel contributed.

"And, I would love it if you would call me Mom," Ruth supported what Samuel said.

Now that wonderful smile that Billy used so infrequently came across his face when he said, "Okay." Then he added one more question, "Do you think Terry will know I'm part of the family now?"

Ruth chuckled as she responded to his question, "I think Terry already thinks you are part of the family."

Samuel then picked him up and gave him a giant bear hug swinging him around until he started to giggle non-stop.

Soon they were all giggling as Ruth said, "Billy, welcome to our family."

Samuel finally put Billy down and said, "Alright, I can smell the coffee and I'll bet Billy would love a glass of milk with his cookie, am I right?"

Billy quickly answered, "Yes I would like a glass of milk and one of those chocolate chip cookies Grandma Becker made. They're great."

Ruth got up and said, "Okay then, what are we waiting for let's go."

They all started toward the door. As they did, Billy took one last look at his new décor and left with a regained sense of belonging.

Downstairs the girls and grandparents were already sitting around the kitchen table having their cookies, coffee and milk when Billy, Ruth and Samuel arrive. Martha and Rachel were busy telling their grandparents about the attic adventure and didn't pay attention to their entrance.

Billy grabbed a cookie and a glass of milk already poured for him and stood over by the counter. Samuel came over by Billy and stood next to him putting his arm around Billy's shoulders.

"Listen everyone, I have an announcement to make," Samuel said causing everyone's head to turn towards him. "Ruth and I just had a special conversation with Billy and we asked him to be part of our family. We are going to adopt him."

Looking at Martha and Rachel, who were looking a little confused, Samuel added, "And, Billy is going to be your big brother and be able to play with you and do things around the farm with you anytime you want."

Martha spoke as if chiding her father, "Daddy, we already do that."

Samuel looked directly at Ruth who was smiling intensely and said, "Well then, I guess things will just keep going normally as Billy continues to be part of our family."

Samuel then patted Billy on the head and walked over to stand by Ruth to have his coffee and cookie. He gave Ruth a quick kiss on the cheek, an unusual move for someone who rarely shows outward emotion.

All of the grandparents said they were very happy with the decision and welcomed Billy to the family. Soon everyone was back to chattering about little things and big things, whatever came to mind. Things were back to normal, for everyone except Billy. He was feeling a new excitement he never felt before as he finally felt at home knowing he belonged.

As Billy looked around the room at everyone he decided he had found the greatest treasure of all, this new family of his. They were in their own world and he was now officially part of it. They all cared about him and loved him. He knew that now.

Billy also understood that God really was looking out for him and taking care of him, when all seemed lost. He decided, at that moment, that he would say a special prayer of thanks to God for his new family, when he said his bedtime prayers.

Never could he have imagined such a dream come true. This was more than one of his imaginary adventures this was real. The hurt Billy felt from his father and grandmother's rejection was now overshadowed by the love he was being given by the Schultz family. He felt safe in the knowledge that his new family would love and care for him forever. He didn't have to leave and he no longer had to worry about his future. He could barely contain his excitement. Billy knew the treasure was a gift and he would never forget it.

*If you have been touched
by this story of Christian love,
please consider passing this book
on to your family and friends.*

CPSIA information can be obtained at www.ICGtesting.com
Printed in the USA
236071LV00002B/3/P